One Week of You

ONE WEEK OF YOU

A NOVEL

LISA WILLIAMS KLINE

Lisa Williams Kline

Goldenjay Books

Publisher's Cataloging-in-Publication Data
Kline, Lisa Williams.
One Week of You: A Novel.
p.____ cm.____
ISBN 978-1-947834-34-7 (Pbk.), ISBN 978-1-947834-33-0 (Ebook)
1. Young Adult Fiction. 2. High School Fiction. I. Title
813.6 | LOC PCN 2018959348

Goldenjay Books

Published by Goldenjay Books
an imprint of Blue Crow Publishing, LLC
Chapel Hill, NC
www.bluecrowpublishing.com
Original Cover Art & Design by Lauren Faulkenberry

PRAISE FOR ONE WEEK OF YOU

Kline has a gift for writing complex characters and creating stories with a beating heart.

-EMILY SMITH PEARCE, AUTHOR OF *ISABEL AND THE MIRACLE BABY* AND *SLOWPOKE*

In *One Week of You*, Lisa Williams Kline perfectly channels the inner workings of the young adult mind, complete with every quivering ounce of angst, fear, and self-doubt.

-FRANK MORELLI, AUTHOR OF *NO SAD SONGS*

Achingly true to new love in all its confusion and comedy, and even its moral complexity.

-CLAUDIA MILLS, AUTHOR OF *ZERO TOLERANCE*

Kline has adroitly combined all the ingredients of a heartfelt coming-of-age story with an enticing mystery— and there's plenty of humor and poignant life lessons baked right in.

- JOHN J. BONK, AUTHOR OF *MADHATTAN MYSTERY, DUSTIN GRUBBS: ONE-MAN SHOW*, AND *DUSTIN GRUBBS: TAKE TWO*

CONTENTS

For Caitlin and Kelsey

CHAPTER ONE

SO, here's how it happens:

I'm standing outside Lakeside High after freshman cheerleading practice waiting for my older brother Ryan. I'm always one of the last to get home because Ryan is the last person to leave yearbook staff every day.

And I'll always remember this: Some guy standing behind me is playing "Skinny Love" on his phone and singing along at the top of his lungs. He doesn't have a good voice at all, in fact his voice is terrible, but he has an incredible amount of out-of-tune enthusiasm, and I can't help it. I turn around, smiling.

It's Andy Masters. Andy Masters, the chief roving reporter for WLHS, the Lakeside freshman class video news program. Andy Masters, the Clown Prince of the ninth grade. Andy Masters, the exciting new guy who just moved to our lakeside town of Mooresville, North Carolina in January and is in my Health class but has never noticed me once.

"I'm a great singer, right?" he says with a grin.

"Very enthusiastic," I agree, still with my ridiculous smile. Even having a short conversational exchange with him is enough to give me hives. Talking to him feels like plugging into an electromagnet. I turn back around, my face feeling hot, and my mind blanking about what to say next. Maybe nothing. Probably our exchange will be over.

But no. Andy pokes me on the shoulder. I turn back around.

"Do I know you?" he says. He's a skinny guy, with so much energy it seems to fly from his fingertips and off the ends of his dark curls. It's like I'm being caught in a vortex.

I feel like a searchlight has been turned on me. "Lizzy Winston. We're in Health class together. I sit three rows behind you." Has he not heard Ms. Robinson call my name every day during attendance since class started three months ago?

"We are?" Andy's green eyes are wide behind his wire-rimmed glasses. He has eyelashes a girl would die for. He seems knocked over by disbelief.

"We are."

"Well, then, I'm definitely going to need your number."

"You are?"

He grabs his head as if he can't believe how obvious this is. "Duh! In case I need to contact you about Health homework!"

"Oh!" I burst out laughing.

"Do you think we're ever going to *have* Health homework?"

Why can't I stop giggling? I give him my number. It's the first time a boy has ever asked.

SUNDAY

It's ten o'clock at night and I'm lying in bed texting Marisa. We have this game we play. She knows I want to be a doctor, so she started making up fake diseases that she's sure she has and texting me about them. "I-can't-focus-on-homework disease." "Snarfing down-potato-chips disease." Stuff like that. Now we both do it.

I have AMSD, I type.

What's that? she replies, playing the game.

Andy Masters Smiling Disease.

Haha.

Every time I think about him I start smiling and can't stop.

Only an hour after I got home Friday, Andy texted me. **I am really good at singing basically anything,** he wrote.

I texted back, **I bet, LOL.**

We've been texting back and forth all weekend ever since. I've been trying to think up witty answers to his funny texts. Or writing answers to him and saving them. Rewriting them. Sending them to Marisa to see what she thinks. Then being afraid I accidentally sent them to the wrong person. Realizing I had way too many "LOL's." Deleting them.

You have to stop me, I text Marisa. **I'm obsessed**.

So? She answers. **What's wrong with that?**

I said I'd never be obsessed with a guy!

Two summers ago, after seventh grade, my old best friend Kelly and I swore we would not be like other girls and make fools of ourselves over guys. We swore we'd stay focused on being doctors. And, until now, there had not been any boys to make a fool of myself over.

Well, stuff happens. ;)

Marisa, my new best friend, whose boyfriend Cody seems crazy about her, clearly doesn't see a problem with making a fool of yourself over a boy. My brother Ryan says ninth grade boys are only interested in one thing. Does that include Andy?

Then Marisa's next balloon pops up.

Ready to be a 15-year-old mom?
OMG, what??

What is she talking about? Then I remember—April Fools' Day is next week.

I know I'm obsessed with Andy, and I know next week is April Fools', but come on!
No, Lizzy! Did you get your flour baby?

I sit bolt upright. *Oh, no! The week of the flour baby!* It's not April Fools'—it's real! I can't believe I've forgotten. Yes, I can. I forget everything. And, this weekend, since I've started thinking about Andy 24/7, it's even worse.

In my PJs, I sidle down the hall and into Mom's bedroom, gritting my teeth, dreading what I have to say. "Mom? I need a five pound bag of flour for my flour baby for Health class tomorrow."

Mom's propped in bed in her nightgown, reading a biography of someone named Marie Curie. She's always reading biographies of outstanding people. She probably wishes I were a more outstanding person. She rubs her eyes, which look tired. She runs a pale hand through her dark hair, which is showing gray because she's trying to save money on hair appointments. "Elizabeth! You're telling me I have to take you to the grocery store now?"

"Well, you did have half a bag of flour in the pantry but when I moved it a moth flew out."

Mom was never big on baking. Since she lost her job, she's basically allergic to the kitchen. "So, what's wrong with the occasional moth fluttering out of your flour baby? It adds interest."

"Mom!"

She leans her head back against the pillow and closes her eyes. "Lizzy, I was at the grocery store this afternoon. Why didn't you tell me this before?"

"I...forgot." I wish I could talk to Mom about Andy. The guys who have been in school with me all these years never notice me at all. Only a new guy would notice me. What does that mean?

"Can't Ryan take you?"

"He's at that *Lord of the Rings* movie marathon down at Birkdale, remember?"

"That's right." Mom squints at the clock on her nightstand and groans. "And who knows when your father will be home? Those Red Cross board meetings last forever. " She jams the cap on her pen and tosses it onto the faded bedspread. "You must be the most forgetful person in the entire ninth grade."

I look at the floor. Neither one of us mentions the thing I forgot on Friday afternoon after I started that text-fest with Andy. It's like the Loch Ness Monster, slithering through the cold depths below the water's surface. Seconds pass. Mom takes a deep breath and then pulls on sweat pants and a sweatshirt over her nightgown.

I yank some jeans and a top on, pull my dark blond hair into a ponytail, and glare at myself in the mirror, mad at my forgetful self. I'm wearing my Coke-bottle glasses because I took my contacts out. My squinty eyes look just like Mom's and my ski jump nose makes it impossible for anyone to take me seriously. I follow her out to the garage.

It's normally warm in North Carolina by the first of April, but this year it's especially hot, and when we back out of the garage in the dark, the air feels amazingly soft. An iris has bloomed at the end of the driveway, and the dogwood in the yard is bursting with flowers. Our next door neighbor's boat is in the driveway, parked after a Sunday on the lake. In our town there are the houses that are on the water, and the houses that aren't. Ours isn't. Still, seeing the boat makes me feel like summer is closer, and I'm more hopeful about everything. So I try joking with Mom on the way to the store.

"They think that carrying around a bag of flour that's supposed to be a baby will keep us from having sex," I say. "*Helloo!* If I were planning on doing it, I don't think a bag of flour would swing me the other way."

"I'll swing you." Mom glances at me. "Stay away from men!"

Men? Andy's fifteen. Is that a man?

"I'm serious, Elizabeth, you better not even think about *kissing* a boy until you have your Ph.D. Or medical degree. Or whatever." The street lights overhead shine down on Mom's face, making her skin look like bluish marble, like a sculpture carved by Michelangelo, or one of the faces on Mount Rushmore. "I've had so much trouble getting a job these past few months, with all these cutbacks. I want you to have "doctor" in front of your name. Messing around with some boy will totally ruin that."

See? The thing is, I feel exactly the same way. I feel like wanting to become a doctor has been part of me ever since I can remember. And now, it's like I'm going behind my own back to go against everything I've always believed. And there's no point in bringing it up to Mom because I already know exactly, word for word, what she will say.

Having an older brother means that I've found out the truth about a lot of things before I wanted to. I found out that kids who used to focus on trying to win the North Carolina Science Fair and collecting food for the needy hit high school and morph into monsters who steal beer out of people's garage refrigerators, inhale computer cleaner, and throw Nikes over electrical wires at intersections. And, of course, they fool around. It's like the people who passionately swore during fifth grade drug awareness training never to smoke or drink or fool around are kidnapped, and they're replaced by aliens who are totally obsessed with doing all of those things.

Well, now I'm in high school. Next year I'll move from the protected freshman hall at Lakeside High to the full-fledged high school. The place where my goal will be to focus like a laser beam on my grades. Where I will need to work hard to excel in biology and chemistry and physics. Sometimes I break out in a sweat just thinking about it.

But now, Andy's flirting with me. And I want to flirt back. Is there some crazy little twin inside me sneaking around, plotting to do stuff that the rest of me is completely against? It seems like this would be one of the main things a girl could discuss with her mom.

But not mine. Not since what happened on Friday, anyway.

———

Mom stands in the flour aisle with her nightgown hanging out from below her sweatshirt. Under the fluorescent grocery store lights the bags under her eyes look huge. Before she lost her job, she cared about her looks. She wore lipstick and eyeliner and had stylish caramel streaks in the front of her dark hair. I stare at the floor. If it weren't for me, maybe she'd have a new job.

"Which one do you want?" she says.

"Huh?"

"Let's see...There's whole wheat. Your flour baby could be a health nut. What about Gold Medal? Your flour baby could win an Olympic event."

"Purple," I say, hoping she'll stop. I point to a generic brand of flour in a pale purple package.

"Perfect," Mom says. "Gender non-specific." She speed-walks toward the checkout counter. "Now, Elizabeth, you've got to keep track of this flour baby. You've got to get an A in Health to stay on honor roll. Everything counts this year."

"Mom, I think I can keep track of a bag of flour. I'm going to babysit for my first real baby this weekend." I've babysat for older kids, but Casey will be the first baby.

"Lizzy, are you kidding? You'd forget your head if it wasn't attached."

A flush of anger creeps up my neck. "For your information, Casey's mom called and asked me for Saturday night."

Mom looks at me, wide-eyed. "Oh, Lizzy, I heard that baby had colic."

"What's that?"

"They cry all the time. Especially between the hours of seven and ten."

"Oh, no." I'm supposed to babysit from 6:30 to midnight. My stomach sinks. The sound of a baby crying makes me so upset sometimes that I cry, too. But another part of me, the part that wants to be a doctor, wonders what causes the crying and what can be done to cure it. I'll look it up on my phone as soon as we get back to the car.

"I just don't know if you can handle a colicky baby, Lizzy." Mom shoots me an intense and doubtful look.

"Mom! Yes, I can!" I cannot believe she has so little faith in me and it makes me so mad I wish I could go out and become a doctor tomorrow just to prove to her that I can. Mom and Dad held me back a year before kindergarten. I was a preemie and always really small for my age. So I'll be sixteen this summer, a year older than most of my classmates. But Mom still thinks of me as a preemie, I think. It drives me crazy.

"Well, you've already said 'yes,'" Mom is saying. "And maybe he's outgrown it."

"Outgrown what?"

"Colic. Anyway, your forgetfulness has already had enough of an impact on this family."

My face heats up and I bite my lip. "Mom, please." The tape starts again, of me texting with Andy on my phone Friday afternoon, and the house phone ringing. Mom and Dad have talked about getting rid of the landline, but they never seem to get around to it. When I answered it, a lady asked for Mom. She said Mom was being called back for another interview. But, because I was in a hurry to get back to Andy, I didn't write it down. And I forgot to tell her. Mom missed the call-back for Iredell County's only open library job.

Talk about mad.

"If I don't get a job, a lot of things are going to have to change around our house. Your cheerleading, for example. We won't be able to afford it next year."

"I know." Mom has already told me this.

"I don't know why you want to be a cheerleader, anyway, Lizzy. You're too smart for that."

I think about saying, "So, all cheerleaders are dumb?" Or I could be honest, and say, "I'm tired of being a science geek, what's wrong with being part of a fun team, wearing a cute uniform, practicing together every afternoon, feeling like I belong to something? Besides, I'm short. It's not like I'm going to make the basketball or volleyball team." But, as usual with Mom, I say nothing.

"Plus, with me getting laid off, we've had to raid your college fund. I want you to tattoo 'scholarship' on your forehead."

I swallow and don't say anything. I tell myself she's just mad about her job and having to come back to the grocery store on Sunday night. It's not just me forgetting the phone call.

As Mom counts out change to cover the tax, the checkout

lady asks if we're planning some heavy duty late night baking.

Mom slaps down a few dollars. "The week of the flour baby."

"Ninth grade Health, huh?" The check-out lady gives a gravelly laugh. "I don't think a baby has weighed five pounds in our family in fifty years. We specialize in twelve-pounders with big heads." She scrunches up her face in mock pain.

"Ouch!" Mom says.

I stare at the floor. Oh! I get it. That big head has to come out. That has to be the grossest thing I have ever heard.

"See? What did I tell you?" Mom grabs her receipt and speed-walks to the parking lot. "Stay away from men."

Appropriate time to talk to Mom about Andy? Never.

————

On the way home, as we're crossing the bridge over Lake Norman, the lights blinking on the shore, I look up "colic" on my *Five-Minute Med Consult* app. Apparently doctors don't know what causes it, and it really has no cure. It could be allergies, nervous parents, or taking in air while eating. Great. My Saturday night babysitting job should be just great.

When we pull up to the house, the kitchen light is glowing, which means Dad is home. Mom stays in the garage to organize the recycling and even though I don't want to help her, I think I should, so I start to peel apart a cardboard box.

"No, no, that's not the way I do it, Lizzy," she says irritably. "Just go inside." She yanks the box apart.

Ever since Friday, everything I do is wrong to her. I so want my mom to be proud of me, but sometimes it feels like climbing Mount Everest. With Dad? He's another story. I never worry about whether he loves me. I head into the kitchen, thinking maybe I can ask Dad about Andy. When you like someone else, should you let them know? Or is it better not to? What happened when Dad met Mom?

"Party on, Wayne," I say as I step inside. Dad's name is Wayne and so we use code from that ancient *Wayne's World* skit on Saturday Night Live. I can't ask Dad about Andy, though, because Ryan is sitting at the counter wearing a faded Star Wars T-shirt and eating a bowl of cereal. Dad loosens his tie, then fishes a stack of manila folders from his beat-up leather briefcase. He is on staff at the Red Cross, and part of his job is to run the board meetings. The Red Cross always needs more money and more blood. Listening to Dad talk about his job is one reason I wanted to be a doctor in the first place.

"Party on, Garth," Dad says. He puts the manila folders on the counter, runs his palm over his bald head, and hugs me. "How are you, sweetie? What's the flour for? I know. You're going to make us some of your famous chocolate chip cookies. I always look forward to that." Dad's not very tall, which is why I'm short, I guess, and he stays fit by running and playing basketball with a group of dads.

"No, this week we have to carry around a bag of flour that's supposed to be a baby."

Dad guffaws. "What?"

"Oh, man, I remember that," Ryan says. "Incredibly stupid, that was." Ryan and his friends sometimes talk like Yoda, which is really annoying. Ryan is anti-athletics and has a skinny chest, but has Dad's really soulful eyes. We have the same curly dark blonde hair.

Dad takes the flour from my hands, and turns it back and forth, like a museum object. "If you lose this bag of flour, you've lost a baby?"

"Yeah, Mom thinks I'll lose it."

"I'll take odds," Ryan says with a snort. "Lose mine, I did not."

"Look, I'm not going to lose my flour baby, ok?" I growl.

"Wanna bet?" The back door slams and Mom comes in. Dad hugs her and after a second she gives him an impatient pat on the back and pulls away. She's mad at everyone.

"I know nobody asked me, but I think carrying around a bag of flour like it's a baby is ridiculous," Dad says, ignoring Mom's mood. "What in the world does a bag of flour have to do with a real living being?" He throws the purple bag of flour at me like a pass in basketball and because he was my fourth grade coach (before everyone else got taller than me) I react instantly by grabbing it as it clubs my chest. "Sometimes I think everyone in the world is completely nuts."

"It's part of the curriculum, Wayne. Apparently with all the budget cuts they didn't have enough mechanical babies, so most of the kids have to go with the old-fashioned flour type," Mom explains.

"Yeah, chill, Dad," Ryan says. "I had to do it."

Dad catches my gaze and the annoyance in his eyes melts away. "Forget what I said, sweetie. Your whole life, you're going to find that for one reason or another you're going to have to do stupid things. Carrying this bag of flour around is one of those things. Anyway, Lizzy, go with the program, and don't lose this blasted thing."

"Good luck with that," says Mom.

Dad sighs. "You better get to bed."

I head upstairs to my bedroom, with my purple bag of flour, gritting my teeth over Mom's last remark.

Ryan, right behind me, says, "A million dollars says you lose it the first day."

I grit my teeth even harder. I'm going to show them. I'm going to show them all.

And, starting tomorrow, I'm ignoring Andy. I am not going to make a fool of myself over a boy.

CHAPTER TWO

MONDAY

WE HAVE ASSIGNED seats on the school bus. (And they say this is a free country.) I sit next to my old best friend Kelly, with the purple bag of flour sliding across my lap every time the bus driver makes a turn. Ryan goes to Chess Club before school, which is why I have to take the bus one way. I mean, I could get up at 5:30. But let's be real.

This summer I'm going to get my driving permit. With cheerleading practice there hasn't been time to take Driver's Ed. And there is no car for me to drive even if I could. As soon as I get my license I'll get a work permit—but for now I have to earn my spending money by babysitting.

"So, what's his name?" asks Kelly.

"Whose name?" I say. "Do you mean Andy?" My face goes hot. How did she already guess I liked Andy? In elementary school, Kelly and I would put on our dads' old white dress shirts and play "Operation," pretending to be doctors. Two summers ago, we went together to Camp Med on a college campus near the North Carolina coast, where we had a mock OR, learned CPR and the Heimlich maneuver, and learned how to use a stethoscope, among other things. Ever since then I've wished I could get a chance to use CPR or the Heimlich maneuver to save someone's life, but it's never come up. That was when Kelly and I made our pact never to make fools of ourselves over boys. But last spring, at the end of eighth grade, I made the freshman cheerleading squad and Kelly joined the Women in Science Club. Kelly says that cheerleading has artificially raised my social status and that being in Women in Science has artificially lowered hers, but this injustice will be righteously corrected when we're adults. Anyway, obviously, we're not as close as we used to be. She is absolutely the last person I'd tell that Andy and I texted all weekend.

"No, I meant what's your flour baby's name?" Kelly is black, and she wears her hair straight, always in a perfect bun. She wears her hair just like our idol, Dr. Sharon Parker, who is the primary care physician for both of our families. Kelly wears a scrub top to school almost every day with her jeans. Her mom, who's a physician's assistant, gets them for her. "But are you saying you like Andy Masters?"

I stare at her, wishing I could duct tape my mouth shut.

"Andy Masters, the newest, the most popular guy in the ninth grade?" she goes on. "Andy Masters, the host of *The WLHS Show*? Andy Masters, who lives in a house that looks like a castle? Don't you think he's out of your league?"

Out of my league? Did she really say that?

I'm sure Kelly thinks that now that I hang out with Marisa and the other cheerleaders, I've turned shallow. I am still smart. I do still want to be a doctor. But is it a crime that I want to be a cheerleader, too? Cheerleading is not what people think. It's about practice, and teamwork, and belonging to something. I really can't put into words the feeling I get when we put our hands together in the middle of our circle before we compete and yell "Wildcats!" Or the way it feels when we all sing "Uptown Funk" by Bruno Mars at the top of our lungs on the bus on the way to our competitions.

"You think Andy is out of my league?" I repeat.

Kelly shrugs. "It *is* April Fools' week. Do you?"

"Wait, you think he's texting me as an April Fools' prank?" Angry heat burns my cheeks. "Kelly, *that is so mean!*"

She waves a fluttery hand. "Lizzy, can't you take a joke? That was just a joke!"

Was it?

Maybe I do pinch myself when he texts me. And maybe on Friday when he gave me that funny electric smile I did look over my shoulder to see if he was smiling at someone else. I start to tell her that I can't believe she came out and said that—but then the bus stops at the entrance to a lakeside neighborhood and Harrison gets on.

"I got ruthenium!" he announces to the entire bus as he swings into the seat behind Kelly and me.

"Then don't sit with me!" someone yells.

It's useless to hope he won't try to talk to us, but still I do. Short and thin, with pale white skin, stick-straight dark hair, and tortoiseshell glasses, Harrison is obsessed with his collection of periodic elements. Last week, he told us he has a display table in his basement and one by one is assembling samples of every element. He is already taking Calculus with a bunch of juniors. There's not a freshman class that's advanced enough for him.

He leans over the seat. "Ruthenium was discovered in Russia in 1844 by Karl Karlovich Klaus."

No one responds, and he doesn't notice Gordon, the stocky black kid in the seat behind him, grinning uncontrollably as he sticks a piece of chewed gum to Harrison's backpack. Gordon's mom died last year of cancer, and even though Gordon made the baseball team his father has not yet been able to get over his grief enough to come to the games.

"My flour baby doesn't have a name yet," I say to Kelly. "I think it's a girl."

Behind us, Harrison snickers. "Lizzy, you do know that there are scientific methods for determining the sex of a child."

He eavesdrops on everything we say on the bus. Can't he sit somewhere else?

I want to be nice to him. Dad's most repeated line as a parent, his most important teaching to Ryan and me throughout our lives, has been, "Be nice to everyone." So I feel guilty about how I feel about Harrison.

"Mine is named Marie Curie." Kelly shows me her bag of flour decorated with a braided cinnamon bun. I guess Marie Curie, whoever she is, has a bun. Taped to her flour baby is a test tube with a button-sized flashlight inside. Isn't that the same person Mom's book is about?

"Marie Curie—discoverer of radium and polonium! One of my heroes!" crows Harrison. "Awesome!" Harrison's flour baby is dressed like Einstein, decorated with picked-apart cotton balls, forming bushy white hair, eyebrows like whirligigs, and a lopsided mustache. And he's scribbled "E =mc2" all over it. I would rather die than ask him anything about it; it would probably take three weeks to get myself out of the conversation. Kelly says to ignore him. I hope Dad understands.

As we're getting off the bus, I get a text from Andy.

Morning dizzy Lizzy. Tell me you can't wait to see my show. **(blushing smiley face)**

He's right, I can't wait. My heart speeds up.

But I put my phone away. First, I'm trying to quit answering him. Second, I don't want Kelly to see.

Thirty minutes later I'm sitting in homeroom with my purple bag of flour on my desk, waiting for *The WLHS Show*. The minute I see Andy's face, with his lively green eyes and mysterious grin, I get this uncontrollable urge to smile.

"It's official, we are now entering April Fools' week, and we have no idea what kinds of pranks are going to be coming down, so don't let down your guard!" Andy points at the sign on the door to the guys' bathroom just behind him. "Heads up—there might be extreme challenges to taking care of our bodily functions. Have the signs on the bathroom doors been switched? Has somebody put clear cling wrap over the toilet seat? And if there was ever a time to look for a whoopee cushion before you sit down in the cafeteria, this is it! Not only that, it's the dreaded week of the flour babies." On-screen Andy continues, his skinny frame walking down the hall toward the camera. "Almost every ninth grader in the school has one." He stops and holds out the microphone to Brian Williams, who stands by his locker. Andy has so much nervous energy, he seems to create a whirling aura that follows him around. "Hey, Brian, show us your flour baby."

Brian is a football player who dresses very prep, usually in polo shirts and khakis. Ever since his parents' divorce, he wears these reflective aviator sunglasses so you can never see his blue eyes. His flour baby wears a tiny ripped black T-shirt and has safety pins poking through its drawn-in ears, nose, eyebrow, and lower lip.

A thin stream of flour leaks out from the nose piercing. Brian swipes the escaping flour away, and, when it cakes his hands, he wipes them on his pants, leaving soft white handprints. Everyone in homeroom laughs.

"Runny nose?" Andy observes.

"Yeah," Brian agrees, laughing.

"Your flour baby sprung a leak. Will that, like, affect your grade?"

"I don't know, man."

"Basically you've stuck a bunch of holes in your flour baby."

Andy holds up a roll of duct tape and loudly rips off a piece for Brian. "Here." Brian laughs and tries to stick the tape onto his flour baby. The tape gets stuck to his hands and the flour baby leaks a little more. Andy rips three more pieces and now they are both laughing out of control. While frenzied violin music plays in the background, they tape up the flour baby. Finally, Brian lifts the flour baby aloft, with duct tape X's everywhere. Andy turns to the camera. "Until tomorrow this is Andy Masters." He does his signature sign-off, which is knocking on his own curly head three times, and then adds, "Mastering reality one day at a time."

I can't stop laughing. I swear Andy's energy field pulls me in like a planet pulls a moon. I take out my phone.

You're hilarious, I type, before I can stop myself.

Andy Masters Smiling Disease (AMSD). No known cure.

———

Later that morning, in Health class, I look for Andy, but he's not there. I promise myself that I'm not going to worry about where he is or check to see if he's texted me. I've noticed a kind of fluttery, dull ache in my stomach today. When I look it up on *Five-Minute Med Consult*, I learn that it could be appendicitis, pancreatitis, endometriosis, gas, or nerves. I immediately reject gas and nerves as being too boring. What if it's appendicitis? Unfortunately the nurse is only at our school on Tuesdays and Thursdays (because of cutbacks), so I could be on my own here.

I try to distract myself and notice that beside me, Marisa has dressed her flour baby like an anime character.

"I like her eyes," I say. "Really big and expressive."

"Yeah, it's from the series about the psychic girl." Marisa flips her glossy dark hair behind her shoulder. Marisa Tanaka's father is Japanese and her mother is white. She has flawless, light brown skin, and she's the best tumbler on our cheer squad. Her parents used to want her to be a top-level gymnast, but she put her foot down in seventh grade and convinced them that she wanted a normal life. But she's still really driven in school and sports and stuff. I guess you don't just forget that kind of discipline.

Other girls have dressed their flour babies in doll clothes. A few guys have put knit caps and sunglasses on theirs. Dressing up our flour babies was part of the assignment but of course, I forgot. I don't have anything on mine.

"I feel like a total flour baby slacker," I tell Marisa. "Do you have a marker or something?"

Marisa laughs. "Sure. You slacker mom, you!"

She hands me a marker, and I scribble a face on my purple bag of flour, with cartoon eyes and a wobbly wide grin.

"That looks kind of like that cartoon character named Ziggy," Marisa says.

"That's what I'll name it! Ziggy." I can't help but sneak a look around the room.

"I saw that," Marisa says with a grin. "You're wondering where Andy is, right?"

"No, I'm not!" I say, too loudly.

"Right. Hey, I heard a rumor that he's going to invite you to the freshman dance on Friday night."

"Are you serious?" Flirty texting is one thing. Going to the freshman dance is another. If he invites me...what does that mean?

"Welcome, people, to flour baby week." Ms. Robinson, the white lady who has been teaching Health at Lakeside High for twenty years, paces the front of the classroom. Tall, gawky, pale-skinned and white-haired, she straightens her wire-rimmed glasses on her beakish nose. She looks like a stork.

Andy comes to the doorway with a pink excused tardy slip in one hand and a flour baby with a backward blue baseball cap in the other. Marisa pokes me with her foot and raises her eyebrows.

"Have a seat, Andy."

He hands her the pink slip and weaves back to his seat.

"Now," Ms. Robinson continues, "because of the shortage of mechanical babies, those of you who remembered to turn in your permission slips first were the ones who got them."

That would not be me. I am never the one who remembers to turn in her permission slip first.

Andy raises his hand. "Ms. Robinson, as a journalist, I feel the need to question the status quo on occasion. What's the point of us carrying around a bag of flour?"

Ms. Robinson stalks to the board, and picks up a marker. She writes, in big letters, RESPONSIBILITY. "That's the point, Andy. When a person has become an adult, and is no longer a child, they are responsible."

"I could be responsible for a real baby," argues Andy. "But who cares about a bag of flour? How many people have babysat for real kids?" He holds out his hands, palms up, appealing to the rest of us.

A bunch of us, some guys but mostly girls, say, "Me!"

"I have a babysitting job this Saturday," I whisper to Marisa. "My first real baby. Casey. But Mom says the baby has colic."

Marisa looks at me, wide-eyed. "What's that?"

"They cry all the time. Especially between the hours of seven and ten."

"Something you'd like to share with the rest of the class, Lizzy and Marisa?" asked Ms. Robinson.

"No, ma'am, sorry," we say.

"If it were up to me," Ms. Robinson continues, "everyone would have a mechanical baby, but with all the budget cuts that's impossible. So it's the flour babies. It is what it is. Does anyone have any more questions?" She doesn't look like she wants to answer any and no one asks. "OK, people, let's talk logistics. Your flour baby must, and I repeat must, remain with you at all times. In the bathroom, at the game, at the mall." She writes, in large capital letters on the board, "AT ALL TIMES." She recaps the marker and turns to face the class. "One young man who will remain nameless left his flour baby on the bleachers after a soccer game and then it rained. It became a very large, hard biscuit."

Half-hearted laughter fills the room.

"Flour babies have been found in the bathroom, on the bus, under the seats at the movies, at the skating rink, and believe it or not, in the school dumpster. Let's be clear: anyone who loses his or her flour baby gets an automatic zero." For emphasis Ms. Robinson swirls a great big "o" up on the board. "And don't think you can just go out and get another bag of flour. I'm coming around to put my John Hancock on the bottom of every one of your flour babies so I know you have the original." As she says this, she does just that—goes from desk to desk putting her signature in red pen on the bottom of each flour baby.

Andy raises his hand again. "I have a baseball game tomorrow. Can I get my mom to watch my flour baby during the game?"

"Yes, but your mother is perfectly free to charge you an hourly babysitting rate if she wants. If it were a real baby, what would you do with it?" Ms. Robinson scribbles energetically on the bottom of Ziggy and plops him back on my desk.

"I would never have that decision to make," Andy says

matter-of-factly. "Because my dad says if I become a father before I'm thirty, I'm dead."

Everyone laughs. Everyone always laughs at Andy, the new Clown Prince of the Freshman Class. He glances back at me to make sure I'm laughing. Of course, I am.

And Marisa, after watching him glance at me, catches my eye and nods her head as if to say, *See? He likes you.*

"He didn't even know I existed until last Friday!" I whisper to her, and start to blush.

And at that moment the fire alarm peals, jangling loud enough to scramble our brains.

There's a collective gasp as the air molecules in the room seem to stop aimlessly floating and snap into perfectly straight lines.

"We weren't supposed to have a fire drill today," Ms. Robinson says. "This better not be an April Fools' prank." She stands straighter and claps her hands. "Nevertheless. Please follow our fire drill procedure to exit the building in the most orderly and rapid way possible and go to our assigned area. Do not panic."

I glance at Marisa, and we both hold back smiles. Of course it's an April Fools' prank. Ms. Robinson points to Mike Lewis, who sits in the right front desk. "Leave your books, file out QUIETLY. No running, no talking, no fighting."

"What about our flour babies?" I ask.

Ms. Robinson heaves a frustrated sigh and makes an executive decision. "Leave them. We'll just end up with flour flying all over the soccer field."

"But you just told us that we had to take them everywhere," Andy objects.

"I said leave them!" said Ms. Robinson.

This seems pretty crazy, if you think about it. I mean, if you had to evacuate somewhere, and you had a real baby, then of course it would be the first thing you'd grab. But what Ms. Robinson says makes perfect sense. We don't want bags of flour all over the soccer field. So, in a very basic way, here is proof that the bags of flour are not like real babies at all. Just like Andy said.

And on the way out of the classroom, I do what I swore I would not do. I check my phone to see if Andy has texted.

And he has.

A fire drill. Adds excitement to the day! Just like you Miss Lizzy.

I'm not used to getting attention from a boy like this and I have no idea what I'm supposed to do.

CHAPTER THREE

WE RACE DOWN THE STAIRS. The sound of our feet pounding down the stairwell is like a bunch of bass drums. We talk in excited voices. The teachers shush us, lose patience, yell at us, shush us again. A burst of nervous adrenalin makes my kneecaps twitch as I descend.

We stream out the side door and onto the soccer fields. More lines of kids pour from the front door, the back door, and the mobile units. The minute we get out onto the fields the teachers tell us to sit down and to be quiet. Marisa sits next to me. The kids in our Health class sit cross-legged in a circle, amidst other classes scattered like multicolored ants across the field. Teachers flank the goal lines with walkie-talkies. We're camped under a bowl of blue sky while wispy white clouds stream overhead.

Andy, sitting on the other side of the circle, texts me.

Awesome April Fools' prank, do u agree?

A fire engine with red lights whirling and sirens screeching plows into the entranceway and right up over the curb onto the sidewalk in front of the school. Half a dozen firemen in yellow turnouts leap off, gallop up the worn marble steps of Lakeside High, and race inside.

Everyone cheers and claps.

"Quiet!" shouts Ms. Robinson, looking sternly at us.

Two police cars with sirens and lights flashing follow, their doors opening like silver wings as they stop abruptly in front. Four blue-clad cops jump out.

Everyone cheers again as the cops follow the firefighters into our school.

Our cell phones are supposed to stay in our backpacks during the school day, or else they'll get taken away, but we all immediately break them out, assuming a fire drill is an exception to the rule.

"Do not call or text your parents!" says Ms. Robinson. "We are on lockdown and they cannot come get you."

Absolutely no one listens to her.

"Mom? We had to evacuate the school for a fire alarm," Marisa says. "No, I'm OK. I'm fine. We think it's just an April Fools' prank."

Pretty soon, above the rising giddy hum of our voices, there's also the tap-tap-tap of everyone texting like crazy. I text Dad and Mom.

I look around and spot Ryan with his AP lit class over near the bleachers. They are all sitting quietly and looking at their phones. I wave.

The teachers talk on their cell phones, too. Parents want to pick up their kids, but the teachers tell them that they can't. Everyone talks, and the level of noise rises by the second. The rasp of high-pitched gasping tells us that Alison Zinsser has hyperventilated—she does it a couple of times a year—and Ms. Robinson tells her to put her head between her knees.

I look up hyperventilation on *Five Minute Med Consult*. FYI: Usually caused by emotional stress. The light-headedness is caused by a lowered level of carbon dioxide in the blood. Cure? Belly breathing to calm down, or breathing into a paper bag to increase blood levels of CO_2. The head between the knees also works.

Within about ten minutes, a couple of parents pull up outside the school. One of the moms jumps out and runs over to one of the cops, his white, bald head shiny in the sun. The mom's black braids are pulled back in a ponytail, her white blouse crisp. At first we can't hear anything they say, but the cop shakes his head and waves her away.

The mom gesticulates with worry and finally gets back inside her Honda minivan.

We watch the front doors of the school, waiting for the other cops to come out. Surrounded by all the talking kids, the constant shifting sound and movement, I feel like I'm sitting in the surf. Mom and Dad haven't answered my text. Mom is probably still mad about having to take me to the grocery store at ten o'clock last night. Rumors swell and travel like a wave moving to the shore. The minutes float by and the cops and firefighters are still inside our school.

Ms. Robinson makes her way around our circle, handing out DumDum lollipops. "There is something soothing about sucking on a lollipop," she assures us brightly.

I watch everyone stick the lollipops in their mouths, and it occurs to me that this could be a prime time for me to have to do that Heimlich maneuver. All these kids sitting here out on the field. A bunch of them sucking on lollipops. I scan the crowd, trying to be alert, reviewing the steps I'd go through if I had to do it. One, wrap my arms tightly around their abdomen, making a fist with one hand. Two, pull upward and inward sharply. If nothing happens, repeat. I'm pretty sure I've got it down. I could do it.

In the middle of this musing, I get a text from Dad. **What's happened? Everything ok?**

We think it might be an April Fools' prank.

Is Ryan bringing you home?

No, the school is on lock-down. We can't leave or be picked up.

After a few seconds, he writes: **I'm sure it will be ok. Text me every fifteen minutes, ok? Xo**.

Dad is calm like that.

Andy jumps up and runs over to Ms. Robinson. "Can I go down and interview the cops and firefighters for WLHS?"

"Andy, go sit down."

"My hand-held and portable recorder are right in the classroom, I can get them in two seconds."

"Andy, go sit down."

"But if I was a *real* roving reporter—"

"Andy. Go. Sit. Down."

A few classes have brought out their flour babies. Gordon, the baseball player from the bus, and Brian, the preppie football player that Andy interviewed this morning, start tossing them towards each other. When one bursts, everyone starts laughing. Clumps of flour turn the grass white, and a smog of it billows through the air. Brian dumps the rest of his flour baby on Gordon's head.

"You're both getting zeros!" Ms. Robinson yells at the boys, as she dusts the flour off Gordon's head. I think of Casey, the baby I'm sitting for this weekend, and Mrs. Vangraff, his red-haired mom, talking to me about the soft spot on his head, where his skull bones haven't grown together yet. I would never admit it, especially to Mom, but I'm kind of scared about babysitting him, especially after what Mom said about colic. *Five Minute Med Consult* has been so reassuring. (Not). Nobody knows how to cure it. Sometimes rubbing the baby's back or sitting the baby up for feeding helps. The only real cure? Time. Babies usually outgrow it by the time they are a few months old.

Brian and Gordon stop teasing each other and Ms. Robinson marches with them over to Mr. Waggoner, the history teacher. Mr. Waggoner is right out of college, so naturally she talks to him like he's a student. He's also by far the best looking guy teacher at our school. Ryan tells me that half of the senior girls are in love with him, along with all of the female teachers. He's black with sharp, dark brown eyes, tall and fit, with short hair that looks like he gets a haircut every single day. And he dresses like a model from Banana Republic.

But right now, Ms. Robinson is berating him. She must not have a crush on him like everyone else. "Mr. Waggoner, what were you THINKING, letting your class bring their flour babies out here? I instructed my students to leave them in the classroom."

"Well, they're supposed to carry them everywhere," Mr. Waggoner says.

Taking over Mr. Waggoner's class, Ms. Robinson tells the students to line their flour babies up on the soccer bleachers and leave them there. That project takes forever, as a few of the responsible students walk around collecting the flour babies, taking them away from kids who are treating them like footballs, tossing them through the air and letting them get ripped apart. Once the flour babies are lined up on the bleachers, they make me think of the characters from *South Park*. They're so round. Lines of little round people with weird little drawn faces in a rainbow of colors. Stuck there in their rows, the way we're stuck in our circles on the soccer field. Maybe the way we're stuck in our own heads about who we are.

Finally I get a text from Mom. **What's happened? Do I need to come get you**?

Does she sound annoyed?

Can't. We're on lockdown.

Ok. She doesn't sound surprised. **Let me know what happens.**

I hate trying to read her mood through texts.

———

Marisa and I lie in the grass with our heads next to each other, each using one phone earpiece and listening to a playlist. We wait for the firefighters to come out of the school. I sneak a glance over at Andy. He sits in the grass and plays with the laces on one of his shoes, flashing irritated glances at Ms. Robinson.

I wish I knew what he was thinking. I bet he's mad because he can't interview the cops and firefighters. I bet he's trying to figure out a way to do it without Ms. Robinson noticing.

"These kids have so many drills—fire drills, lockdown drills, safety drills.

"Thankfully, so far, nothing has ever happened," Ms. Robinson says to Mr. Waggoner. "The students are not scared. They're just excited to be out of class."

I'm sitting out here under this brilliant blue sky, sucking on a lollipop, and everyone around me chats and laughs.

Wonder who did it.

CHAPTER FOUR

A HALF HOUR later we all jump to our feet as the firefighters and police straggle out the front door and assemble by the flagpole, talking amongst themselves. Surprise, surprise, they didn't find a fire.

The southern drawl of Ms. J, our principal, booms on the loudspeaker, across the parking lots and soccer field. "At this time it is safe for you to return to your classrooms. Please get your belongings, and then wait for a bell to send you to third block."

Ms. J's a tough, older white lady with papery skin and iron gray hair and a last name no one can pronounce quite right. She finally told everybody to just call her Ms. J.

I draw a deep breath as we file through the front doors, heading back inside. Absolutely everyone has theories on who did it.

Back in the classroom, Ms. J, over the loudspeaker, confirms the rumors. "The fire alarm was tripped this morning. We are not sure how it happened, but the fire department and police have ascertained that there is no fire, and that it's safe for us to resume our school day. If indeed this was an April Fools' prank, please be assured that we will find out who did it and that person will be held responsible. In approximately two minutes the bell will ring. We have notified your parents that all is well. Please proceed in an orderly way to your third block class."

As I'm leaving, cradling Ziggy in my arm, I look for Andy. He's not here. Where is he? Will he really ask me to the dance? That pact with Kelly, not to make a fool of myself over a boy, was two whole summers ago. So much has changed since then. Mostly me.

By lunchtime I've already seen one person running down the hall screaming like a banshee, "OMIGOSH I left my flour baby in Ms. Robinson's class!"

I think about how Mom doubted me last night, about the way Ryan bet me a million dollars that I'd lose Ziggy. But look: the day is more than half over, we had a prank fire drill, and I still have Ziggy cradled right here in my arm.

———

Today the smell of formaldehyde curls out the door of the Biology classroom and skulks for yards down the hall in every direction. My eyes burn and my stomach turns over. I wish I hadn't eaten any lunch. Inside the classroom, boys groan and girls are squealing "Ewww."

Once I'm inside, I see why. At each lab station, Mrs. Cruz has placed a tray containing a pinkish-gray fetal pig. All of the classroom windows are open.

Oh, man. I am super-excited to start dissecting the fetal pigs but forgot to get Mom to sign my permission slip. Well, this is definitely something Mom would approve of, right? I know what Mom's signature looks like. Carefully, before I give myself too much time to think about it, I use my left hand to forge

Mom's signature. Then, panicking, I look for Kelly. Even though we're not best friends anymore, we still try to pair up as lab partners in science classes.

With her beautiful silky dark hair, large brown-black eyes, and perfect figure complete with a waist that defies science, everyone agrees Mrs. Cruz is the prettiest teacher in school. Her grandparents came over from Cuba, and she is bilingual. Ryan told me that when she got married last year, all the guys were crushed. But she's very strict, insisting that all students can succeed in science if they apply themselves.

"People, I am excited about this unit!" she tells us. "I worked so hard to get these pigs, but because of budget cuts we weren't able to get as many as I'd hoped, so you will be working in groups of three instead of two." Referring to her clipboard, she calls out the names of people who will be working together. She points at Kelly and me. "The two of you will be working with Harrison."

Kelly and I exchange a horrified look.

"Oh, Mrs. Cruz..." I start.

"Don't even go there." She holds up her hand like a traffic cop.

I sit Ziggy on the lab station, and then put on the rubber gloves. The pig is slightly curled, lying on its side. It could be sleeping. Thank goodness it's not cute. The pig's tightly closed eyes mesmerize me. It doesn't look real, but more like one of those rubber chickens you can buy in joke stores. Formaldehyde stings my eyes. I feel like I'm going to gag. But obviously if I want to become a doctor I have to learn to do this.

Harrison takes forever to maneuver his pale fingers into the medical gloves. "Guess what?" he says. "The next element I'm getting for my periodic table display is going to be rhodium."

"Great," I say.

Kelly rolls her eyes at me, and mouths the word

"obsessed." She snaps the gloves onto her efficient brown hands. "Okay, Lizzy, I'll read the directions and you cut," she says.

"You want me to cut?" My stomach tightens. I was sure Kelly would do it. "You don't want to take turns?"

"You say you still want to be a doctor," she says in a challenging voice. "Prove it, Lizzy." Clearly, she's still holding a grudge about my cheerleading. First the comment about Andy on the bus. Now this.

"Fine," I say, but my stomach lurches. Kelly took care of pithing the frog last semester. I definitely thought she would want to do the cutting.

"What about me?" Harrison says.

"Take notes," Kelly tells him.

Last week we watched videos showing us how to tie the limbs of the pig to the edges of the tray. The tension in my shoulders rises as I struggle with the front legs. Harrison leans close, watching, and he's practically breathing in my hair. His slender whitish hand sits uncomfortably close to mine on the lab station, and his hovering makes me claustrophobic. I pick up the scissors and the probe.

"Harrison, move back a little, I can't see what I'm doing."

"I don't want to miss anything."

"If you just..." I think I might faint if he doesn't give me some space, and finally he leans back a few inches.

I finish tying the rear legs. The fetal pig is not fat; it's so thin its stomach sinks in. Tiny nipples form a double row down the front of its torso like pink buttons on a peacoat.

"Wait," Harrison says. "What should we name it?"

"Name it?" I stare at him in shock and my mouth goes dry. "I don't think we should name it at all."

"What about Wilbur?" he suggests, a smile playing around his mouth.

"No! *Charlotte's Web* is one of my favorite books. I am not naming it Wilbur."

"Babe?"

"NO!" Kelly says. "I loved that movie."

I finally get the pig attached properly. Sweat breaks out on my temples.

"Medical students always name their cadavers," he says.

"I think that's true," Kelly says, without enthusiasm.

I hold out my hand to Kelly. "Scissors."

She slaps them across my palm and we flash smiles at each other, remembering third grade and pretending to do surgery when Mom let the two of us cut up vegetables. Briefly, the tension between us is gone. With growing confidence, I pick up the scissors.

I make a small incision next to the diaphragm, as Mrs. Cruz showed us. The pig is cold and clammy, but I ignore that. I cut upward, toward the pig's shoulders. A liquid—formaldehyde, I guess—spills out and pools on the wax bottom of the tray. I ignore that, too. *C'mon, Lizzy.*

"What about Piglet, like from Winnie the Pooh?" Harrison says.

"No!" I say.

"Are you taking notes, Harrison?" Kelly glares at him.

I have just broken and spread the ribs so we can get a look at the organs when Mrs. Cruz tells us to put the plastic bags over our pigs and start cleaning up. Gosh, it feels like we just got started. I had just gotten the hang of it and now don't want to stop, but I step away from the pig, wiping sweat from my forehead with the back of my gloved hand.

"We'll resume tomorrow," Mrs. Cruz assures us.

"I'll type up my notes and email them to both of you tonight," Harrison says. "What are your email addresses?"

Kelly and I glance at each other. Reluctantly, we scribble our email addresses in his notebook.

As soon as he leaves, Kelly touches my arm, eyebrows raised. "Harrison has a crush on you."

The back of my neck prickles, and I glare at Kelly. "Not me! On you!"

She shakes her head. "Didn't you notice him leaning in and trying to smell your hair when you were cutting into the pig?"

"He said he was just trying to see."

"It's you," she says again.

"No, you," I counter.

She smiles and shakes her head again.

As we leave the classroom, I throw my backpack over my shoulder and pull Ziggy into my arm, thinking with satisfaction that I still haven't forgotten her even though I've had to deal with dissecting a pig and having Harrison breathing all over me. I have *so* got this. Just about made it through the whole first day.

———

On my way to last period, I stop at the water fountain by Ms. Robinson's classroom. I'm leaning to get a drink of water when Andy comes up and drapes his arm over my shoulders and pushes the "ON" button. There's an ice-cold ribbon of water at my service.

"So...I have a question for you." His hair smells like baby shampoo. I realize I'm smelling his hair just like Harrison was smelling mine.

This is it. Marisa was right. He's going to ask me. *What am I going to say?*

"About what?" I play innocent, look up at him and smile. Andy Masters Smiling Disease. Sort of like malaria, or cholera, or one of those other life-threatening things people get.

"So...there's the freshman dance Friday night. Why don't you come, and we can hang out?"

"Wow, it sounds really fun," I say, stalling. But, what does "hang out" mean? My thoughts race. I have to ask my parents. "Can I ...let you know?"

"Hey, what's up? I thought you were into me." Andy says, knitting his brows.

My eyes lock onto his as he scans my face. "I...just have to ask, that's all."

"OK, by Wednesday," Andy says. "After that this offer is null and void and no coupons will be honored. Right now if you could open me up I swear you'd see a broken heart inside. Cracked wide open."

"You seem pretty healthy to me," I poke his chest, starting that idiotic grin again, and trying to escape down the hall.

"Beneath this cool attitude, there's an incredibly sensitive person," Andy says, following me.

"Okay."

"Terrified of rejection."

"Right." My heart does this breathless flutter. I tell it to stop but it's not listening.

He walks backward, does a little electric skip step. "My older brother can take us. He's cool."

"Good to know," I say. Cool about what? "Class," I add, pointing, and pulling away, my idiotic grin getting wider.

"You. Me. Freshman dance. Be there!" He points at me, still walking backward.

I nod, smiling, and tell my heart to please calm down. I stop in the doorway of my classroom.

And I realize—*oh no!*—I don't have Ziggy!

"Andy! You made me lose my flour baby!" I race by him back to Mrs. Cruz's classroom. Did I leave her there? I check the hallway and the bathroom. What did I do with her?

I run back to the gym to check the showers—picturing Ziggy on her way to becoming a pancake. But nada.

Where did I leave her?

I sit on the bench beside the gym lockers, feeling slightly feverish, my heart aflutter, and sneak my phone out of my backpack. I look up heart palpitations on *Five Minute Med Consult*. It says they're usually harmless, caused by stress or exercise. But let's be real, who's to say I'm not having a heart attack?

Mom is going to *kill* me for losing this flour baby. I absolutely hate it when she's right.

Why am I so forgetful?

Normally we avoid looking at ourselves in the cheap full-length mirror beside the gym lockers because it makes us look wavy. I chance it.

I search my face, staring into my own hazel eyes. I look prettier than my past self. I used to be kind of chubby but now I'm skinnier. Not sure how that happened. Maybe cheerleading. Long brownish blonde hair. No glasses, just contacts. I look like a competent, together person. What is wrong with me?

My whole family's prediction has come true. I've lost her.

After school is over I retrace my steps from my entire day without success. I wonder how many hours of my fifteen years I've spent looking for something I have lost. Poor little Ziggy. Where is she?

If I've lost this flour baby, there is no way Mom and Dad are going to let me go to the dance with Andy on Friday night. Even if I was sure I wanted to. Which I'm not.

My hands shake slightly as I shoulder my backpack and head out to meet Ryan who, amazingly, is not late picking me up. I get in, and he waits for me to put on my seatbelt, then carefully shifts the gray Toyota into gear. This is our grandfather's old car—a 1998 Toyota Camry with two hundred and seventeen thousand miles on it.

Everyone at school makes fun of it. Ryan has named it "The Millennium Falcon," after Han Solo's spaceship. He has to be the most careful driver in the universe. Lines of cars bunch behind him on the road. It's so embarrassing. Once he forgot to stop at a stop sign and *backed up* so that he wouldn't be breaking the law. And he says, because of its distracting nature, he won't turn on the radio. I can't even *tell* people that; they'd laugh so hard. And of *course* he would never text.

He glances at my face. "What's wrong?"

I can't tell him.

He stares at me. "Come on, what?"

"I lost Ziggy."

"Who's Ziggy?"

"My flour baby." The words sting my mouth on the way out.

Ryan starts laughing. "I called it! What did I tell you? You owe me a million dollars!"

I am SO mad at myself. "Mom's going to kill me."

A shopping center approaches. My mind races. Suddenly, I can't let this be it. I can't give up on myself this easily. "Ryan, turn here!"

Ryan glances at me, confused. "Why?"

"Please. Park outside the Food Lion. This will only take a minute."

Shrugging his shoulders, Ryan carefully turns the corner and pulls into a parking space. "Don't get out yet, I need to straighten up," he mutters. He backs out and pulls back in, perfectly centered between the lines. "Now, what are we doing?"

I rustle through my purse and somehow find a dollar. "I'm going to get another bag of flour."

"Lizzy, what are you thinking?"

"I saw the way Ms. Robinson puts her signature on the bottom. I can do that. No one will ever know."

Ryan hesitates. "Lizzy, that's cheating!"

"It's not! I'm just giving myself another chance. I'm giving myself more time to find the one I lost. Once I find it I'll get rid of this one." I wait a beat, take a deep breath. I know he's right—it is cheating. But I tell myself it's only *temporary* cheating. "Can you lend me a few dollars?"

Ryan stares at me, drumming his fingers on the steering wheel. "Serious, you are? A time to upset Mom this definitively is not," he finally says slowly. Usually it annoys me when Ryan and his friends talk like Yoda, but today I'm just glad he sees my point. He digs in his back pocket and comes up with a five-dollar bill carefully folded into sixteenths. "I got paid this weekend." He works at the car wash on Saturdays and Sundays. "Okay, go."

I stare at him. "What if somebody sees me?"

"Okay, I'll go." Ryan sighs and swings door open. "Stay here."

The door slams.

"It was the purple one!" I yell after him. "I'll pay you back!" Ryan is a good big brother. He takes care of me. In spite of his skinny chest and permanent cowlick, he does have a good heart. He is a complete Tolkien geek, of course, and he loves T.H. White, who wrote *The Once and Future King* about King Arthur. I want to ask his advice about going to the dance with Andy Friday night.

Ten minutes later, he's back. He tosses a purple bag over to me, then clicks his seatbelt with finality, and turns the key. "We've crossed over to the dark side, you know, Lizzy."

I feel my lip tremble. He's right. I mean, I've never done anything like this. I've practically made straight As all my life. I've never gone to the principal's office. I had perfect attendance until just this year when I had to miss a day with the entire cheer squad to travel to a competition in Raleigh. I don't do things like this.

But I give him my biggest smile. "No, we haven't. It's just a bag of flour. Hey, I want to ask you something."

"What?" At that moment, his ring tone, the theme from Star Wars, goes off. He answers and starts talking to someone from the yearbook committee. My chance to ask him about Andy is gone.

As we pull into the driveway, Ziggy Two, with her newly markered face, rolls under my feet and smushes into the side of the seat. I pick her up and cradle her in my lap. I am going to keep track of her. I swear I am.

"We're home," Ryan and I say as we walk in the house, both checking to assess Mom's mood.

"Hi." Mom dumps a jar of spaghetti sauce into a pan, then points a wooden spoon at me. "Kids, tell me about that prank fire drill. Did they catch whoever did it? How long were you out of class?"

"A couple of hours. No, they didn't catch the person yet. I think the school sent you an email." Mom is not good about checking her email.

"I hope when they catch that little so-and-so they charge him for the cost of the emergency services. Think about the time those firemen and police officers had to spend investigating a prank."

I head toward the stairs. "Yeah."

"Did you find a job, Mom?" Ryan asks.

My face heats up a little. I would never have the guts to ask her that! I can't believe he did.

"No, there are hiring freezes everywhere. I've applied for everything that I'm qualified for, but nothing yet."

A wave of guilt washes over me. If it weren't for me, she'd

have that library job. I start to say how sorry I am about forgetting that message, but Mom barrels on. "So I'm branching out. I have an interview for a job as a forklift driver on Thursday."

"A forklift driver? Cool!" I say.

"Mom, not to sound negative," Ryan says, "but do you *know* how to drive a forklift?"

"No, of course not!!" Mom laughs, but there's an edge to it. "I am not remotely qualified for this job in any way. But I'm a fast learner, and that counts for a lot." Mom swirls the wooden spoon around the pan twice, then points it at me again. "Lizzy, how long did you last before losing your flour baby? An hour?"

I hold Ziggy Two aloft. "Na-nanny-boo-boo."

Ryan studiously examines the stair railing.

Mom's jaw drops open. "Incredible. But, let's be real. It's only been one day."

"Thanks for your faith in me, Mom."

"I just call 'em the way I see 'em. If you manage to keep track of that thing for a whole week, I'll...what will I do? I'll eat a bug."

"Get ready for a bug sandwich on Friday, then!" I say with my teeth clenched. I just can't tell her she was right. I'm going to keep track of this flour baby if it kills me.

———

After dinner Andy sends me a really adorable *YouTube* video of two otters floating along together in the water holding hands. At one point they float apart, but one otter reaches out and takes the other's paw to pull it close again. It's the cutest thing I've ever seen.

Harrison, meanwhile, emails two single-spaced pages of notes describing our dissection. I print them up and stuff them into my Biology notebook without reading them. After that, Andy texts me in French. Since I chose to take Latin, hoping to prepare for "medicalese," I knock on Ryan's door to get him to translate.

"What does this say?"

Ryan turns from the paper he's writing for AP English on famous balcony scenes. He's including Cyrano de Bergerac and *Romeo and Juliet*. I talked him into adding, last but absolutely not least, *Say Anything* with John Cusack. He looks at the screen and translates. "Let's see...you are an adorable little French fry."

"French fry?"

"That's what it says. *Pomme frite*. French fry." He hands my phone back. "Who sent you this, anyway?"

"A guy named Andy. He's the roving reporter for WLHS."

"Roving?" Ryan raises his eyebrows suggestively. "Any person who called me a French fry, my advice would be to avoid."

"I think he's funny. He makes me laugh."

Ryan uses Yoda's throaty voice. "Dangerous, he may be."

"What do you mean, Ryan? Dangerous, how?" I ask. "He asked me to the freshman dance on Friday night. When you were a freshman, did you go to that dance?"

Ryan looks at me. "Knowing me, do *you* think I went to the freshman dance?"

"No."

"You would be correct. I'd rather have needles stuck in my eyes."

"Well, but you and I are different, and I guess I want to know...what do you mean by dangerous? Do you think I should go? I mean, I've had this pact with myself, and with Kelly, that I'd be like a laser beam headed to med school and not get sidetracked by a guy. But I can't stop thinking about him."

Ryan leans forward and scratches his head vigorously with both hands. "Here's the reality: If you lose your flour baby, Mom and Dad will never let you go. If you manage to hang onto it, then maybe they will. My advice would be not to lose that flour baby. Then, wait and ask them on Friday afternoon. Make it a very casual, last-minute thing."

He never did answer my question. What did he mean by *dangerous*?

CHAPTER FIVE

TUESDAY

THE BUS GROANS and shrieks as the driver turns left and pulls into Harrison's neighborhood. My shoulder collides with Kelly's.

The bus grinds to a stop and we can see Harrison through the glass door. When the driver, Mrs. McCready, tries to open the door it won't budge. Harrison stands there waiting, but nothing happens. Mrs. McCready frowns and gives the lever a shove. Gordon, two seats behind us, starts to laugh. Pretty soon everyone on the bus is laughing because the door won't open for Harrison.

Mrs. McCready turns to glare at Gordon. "Gordon, what did you do?"

"Nothing."

"Gordon." Her tone is threatening.

Chuckling to himself, Gordon gets up and climbs down the stairs and tightens one of the bolts on the door. "Okay. It'll work now."

He must have loosened the bolt when he got on and nobody noticed.

When Harrison climbs on, he doesn't even look at Gordon. He pokes me in the shoulder. "After rhodium I'm getting palladium."

"Great, Harrison," I say patiently.

Kelly gives me a warning look. "Ignore him," she mouths. Then she uses her fingers to smooth back her perfect bun and turns on her calculator to work on a math problem.

"That wasn't part of our math homework, was it?" I start to panic, thinking I've forgotten yet another thing.

"Nope. Extra credit," she says.

"Whew." Relief floods me. I tighten my grip on Ziggy Two. Out the bus window I watch two bluebirds fly together from one dogwood tree to another. I wonder if they have a nest somewhere, with a sweet clump of perfectly-shaped eggs that they guard with their lives. I love watching YouTube videos of baby birds pecking their way out of eggs. Or any YouTube videos of animals. Andy sent me one just this morning of two penguins walking along, trying to cross a puddle, talking in English accents. It was hilarious.

"So, did you name your flour baby yet?" Kelly asks.

"Her name is Ziggy."

Behind us, Harrison starts singing tunelessly. "Ziggy, ziggy, boom, boom, ziggy, ziggy, boom boom."

Kelly ignores him, and so do I.

"Ziggy. How are you spelling that?" Kelly's fingers fly over the calculator keys. Marie Curie is cradled under her arm.

"Z-I-G-G-Y."

"Oh." Kelly looks bored and stares out the window.

I wait a second or two. "How else would you spell it?"

"Well, I was thinking of Z-Y-G-G-Y, which has more metaphorical possibilities. As in zygote, you know."

"The stage of fetal development," says Harrison, poking his thin pointy chin between us, "which consists of only one diploid cell, resulting from the merger of two haploid cells—the ovum from the female and the sperm from the male."

"That is pretty amazing, when you think about it. That an entire new person comes from two merged cells?" I can't help but answer him. It is amazing.

"Chemistry," Harrison agrees.

Kelly clears her throat, and cuts her eyes at me in a warning.

I get a text from Andy, but don't want to read it in front of Kelly. So I ignore it.

"Go ahead and look at it. I know who it's from," she says. "You know he's probably going to leave and go to private school next year, so what's the point?"

I hadn't thought of that. "How do you know?"

"Just an intelligent guess." She widens her eyes as if to say "solved."

"Why do you act like me liking Andy is some kind of crime?" I say to her.

"We had a pact, Lizzy!"

"That was a long time ago." Even as I speak the words, I feel guilty.

"Fine," she says.

We both stare straight ahead the rest of the way to school.

———

I am in homeroom, with Ziggy Two on my desk, watching *The WLHS Show* on the monitor in the corner above the door. Andy is interviewing Carrie Rasnik about her flour baby, which is wearing a tiny dog sweater with the signature Freddy Krueger red and green stripe. She's added a smashed fedora, clumps of staples for his teeth, red spots for the pizza face and a pair of sharp kiddie scissors for his hand.

"Whoa," says Andy, into the WLHS microphone. "That is one scary flour baby." I wish I'd been that creative with my flour baby. It seems like Andy is impressed.

Carrie smiles proudly, her competitive side showing. She won the school-wide Halloween costume contest two years in a row. "Isn't he awesome?"

"Absolutely. So what made you decide on Freddy?" He's definitely impressed enough to flirt with her.

Carrie raises her eyebrows. "Well, not many people think about the fact that Freddy was once a baby, too."

"So you'd say he never had a cute and cuddly stage?"

"Never."

"Here's a question: With better parenting, could Freddy have become a tree surgeon and devoted family man?" Andy cannot help smiling at his own cleverness. He stands very close to Carrie.

"I don't think so."

"Thank you, Carrie. This is Andy Masters." He knocks three times on his own head. "Mastering reality one day at a time."

I try to fight off the waves of AMSD as the bell rings and I gather Ziggy Two and my books. Andy was definitely flirting with Carrie. But Andy flirts with everyone. He is just filled with the joy of life. Was Carrie flirting back? AMSD could be highly contagious. Nevertheless, a question scarier than Freddy Krueger sneaks its way unbidden into my brain: Am I the only person that he called his adorable little *pomme frite* last night? Are there flirty texts flying in lots of different directions?

Ms. Robinson's Health class starts again without Andy. I sigh, wishing I didn't pay such close attention to his comings and goings. Why is he late, anyway? Moments later, just like yesterday, he shows up with a pink excused tardy slip.

Ms. Robinson turns on the SmartBoard so we can watch a film depicting the formation of a zygote. I learn that a zygote is then transformed into an embryo by proceeding through first the blastula stage, which is characterized by a fluid-filled cavity called the blastocoel surrounded by a sheet of cells called blastomeres. While I find this all quite fascinating, at the mention of *blasto*coels and *blast*omeres, Andy and some other boys in the back of the classroom cough extra saliva into their mouths and make explosive *blast*ing sound effects.

"Andy, one more disruption and I'll send you out in the hallway," says Ms. Robinson.

Andy nods and looks resigned, but no one is fooled. He isn't a resigned kind of guy, so he's sure to end up in the hallway sooner or later. I realize one of the reasons I like him is that he's such a rebel. I'm not. Getting a second flour baby is the worst thing I've ever done.

In fact, I've never done anything like it and every time I think about it my temples start to throb. What is happening to me?

Ms. Robinson turns to the SmartBoard to change the visual and all of a sudden a cartoon stork appears on the screen. Everyone starts to laugh because the stork looks exactly like Ms. Robinson. Long skinny neck, skinny legs, and the long beak like her nose with the little wire-rimmed glasses. It's a caricature. A really good one. There are only one or two people in the school who can do caricatures like that. One of them is Lance Spock. But how did it get into Ms. Robinson's computer?

"What on earth?" Ms. Robinson sputters. Even in the dark I can see the red of her face.

"Ms. Robinson, it's you!" says Carrie.

"Somebody's hacked your computer!" Andy says.

Before anyone can say anything else, the fire alarm blasts. We jump. The bell's insistent clanging reverberates against the inside of my head.

"Again?" says Ms. Robinson.

Some kids yelp with excitement. Others groan. The relentless peal of the bell, blanketing every corner of our school, makes my head pound. Okay, so there is no doubt now. These are intentional.

"Please follow the same fire drill procedure as you did yesterday," instructs Ms. Robinson. "In the most orderly and rapid way possible."

Everyone stands and rushes for the door.

"Just a minute, stay in order!" Ms. Robinson waves one hand, reaching into her desk to grab the bag of Dum-Dum lollipops with the other.

"Ms. Robinson, I have to get an interview!" Andy jumps up and down like a basketball player trying to tap in a lay-up.

"Andy, get in line."

"Come on, please? I'm a roving reporter! This is the biggest story of the year!"

"Andy, in line! Now!"

He throws his reporter's notepad to the floor.

"Okay, that's it, Andy. You have after school detention tomorrow."

"I've got to investigate the hacking! You can't send me to detention!" He roars with frustration and grabs his head in his hands. I wish I could say something to him, because I feel like Ms. Robinson isn't fair to him. He is filled with the passion of life and she just doesn't see that.

Now we crowd once again into the stairwell, our collective footsteps pounding.

Lance Spock descends the stairs a few steps in front of me. He's always eating alone in the cafeteria when I walk by. He wears a ski hat every day, even in the summer. I cut my eyes at him, catch a glimpse of a dragon he's drawn on his forearm. Was that stork on Ms. Robinson's screen his artwork?

Two steps below me is Chelsea, a girl who hangs with the Goths, with her tiny nose stud, her torn black jeans, and black fingernails stark against her pale white skin. She looks so tough but she was in my second grade class and one day her cat got run over and she cried for the whole day. No matter how many years go by I remember Chelsea as heartbroken. Marisa told me that now Chelsea lives with her dad and he won't let her have a cat.

Brian, the football player who was interviewed by Andy, and then later was throwing the flour babies around at the first fire drill, passes me on the stairs, going the opposite direction of everyone else, mysterious behind his reflective aviators. Well, that's weird.

Then, like a friendly snake, someone's arm drapes over the back of my neck. I gasp and grab the handrail to keep from tumbling down the steps. Then I realize that I've gotten so used to carrying my flour baby that I've accidentally brought Ziggy with me.

"Lizzy, I need your help." Andy's mouth is so close I feel warmth in the hollow of my ear. "I need to get back inside the school, and I need you to provide a diversion."

"What?" My heart twists. "I'm...not exactly the diversionary type," I say. "Far from it, in fact." I shift Ziggy higher on my hip.

"But you are, because you have those awesome cheerleader skills, Miss Lizzy. When we get on the field, if you could just get Ms. Robinson's attention by doing a few flipperinos and twisteroos, I can take care of the rest."

"You mean back handspring back tucks? Or full twisting lay-outs?"

"Yeah, yeah, whatever, that sounds good."

I wish he had more respect for tumbling terms. "Uhh..."

"I know you can do it. You're the best, Miss Lizzy. Miss Tin Lizzy." He hops down the stairs, chanting as he lands on each step, dragging me along with him. "Liz the whiz. Liz the fizz. Liz, you have me in a tizz. Lizzy, Lizzy, you make me dizzy."

Andy Masters Smiling Disease is full-blown now. In fact it's become an acute case of the Andy Masters Helpless Laughing Disease. I'm so very weak I cannot even talk, which means I cannot, certainly, say "no" when he asks me again about the illegal twisterinos and flipperoos.

Can I?

"Just as soon as she does her head count, go out and do your stuff, OK?" he says.

I nod, my neck feeling wooden. When his arm leaves my shoulders a cold breeze slides across my skin, leaving goosebumps in its wake.

So, what does Andy need to get back inside the school for, anyway?

We're out on the field again, with the teachers standing on the spray-painted yard lines with their walkie-talkies. Ms. Robinson gives out lollipops to keep us quiet again, like we're two-year-olds, and the fire engine and cop cars roll up again, slower than yesterday, and without sirens this time. The red and blue lights turn round and round, silently flashing. The firefighters and police trudge up the marble steps.

Ms. Robinson moves her lips silently as she counts us, one hand on her hip. She holds up the green laminated card showing that all students are accounted for. Andy, who has purposely sat directly behind Ms. Robinson, glances at me now, his eyebrows like a drawbridge. This is it, time for my diversion. Heat rises to my cheeks. My fingers start to tremble. I can't do it.

I press my fingers into fists. *Do it now. Andy is counting on you. Do it right now.*

I place Ziggy carefully on the grass. I will come right back and get her. And before I chicken out, I jump up, race to the empty strip of grass between our class and the next, and reel off three back handspring-back tucks and finish with a perfect twisting lay-out.

We cheerleaders are like Pavlov's dogs; when one of us does a back-handspring back-tuck, the rest of us have to jump up and do one, too. And so Tanya and Marisa both jump up, get in line behind me, and each reel one off. I'm such a goody-goody, I can't believe I've started this back handspring-back-tuck revolution! We are flipping and twisting, our bodies sliding like corkscrews through the air, and everyone around us laughs and applauds.

Ms. Robinson storms across the field, almost stepping on people's ankles and thighs. "Ladies! What in Heaven's name are you doing?"

As I reel off the most glorious twisting lay-out of my life, a lay-out that makes me feel like I'm a bullet catapulting through space with a backbone as flexible as a spiral noodle, I can't help letting my eyes slip over to catch Andy skulking across the goal line, and around the back corner of the school. A thrill runs up my spine.

Ms. Robinson grabs my arm. "Elizabeth Winston, I cannot imagine what came over you. You will not leave my side for the rest of our time out here and I personally will escort you to the principal's office the moment they reopen the school." Her thumb and forefinger dig into my elbow. "Marisa and Tanya, I can see she was the ringleader. You all take your seats."

She drags me over to the spot where the teachers stand with their walkie-talkies. "Stand here. Don't go anywhere, young lady."

I have been forgetful. I have been spaced-out. I have done bad things by accident. But never, have I ever, in my life, done something bad ON PURPOSE. And I'm amazed to find that, while guilt creeps along my scalp like a centipede, also surging through me like a locomotive is adrenalin from the pounding of my runaway heart.

I look across the field and see Kelly sitting with her advanced world history class, staring at me with her mouth hanging open, like she can't believe the person I've become. I avoid looking for Ryan because I don't even want to see his face.

Marisa shares her earbuds with someone else while I stand next to Ms. Robinson, my cheeks glowing, for what seems like several hours. She and Mr. Waggoner hold their walkie-talkies and chat as if I'm not there. I wonder if they're going to call my parents about this.

"There is no chance of actually getting any instruction done today," says Ms. Robinson with a sigh.

"The boy who cried wolf," intones Mr. Waggoner.

Finally, the firemen and cops wander across the front yard, and say a few words to each other. One claps another on the back. Another touches his index finger to the brim of his cap as he climbs into the shotgun seat. The others wave, and without lights, without sirens, the fire truck and one cruiser glide away. The other cruiser stays in place.

The bell rings to sound all clear, and then, class by class, we file back into the school. When we arrive back in the classroom, neither Ms. Robinson nor Andy are anywhere to be seen.

"Attention students," says Ms. J over the intercom. "Once again, our dedicated firefighters and police have determined that there is no fire on the premises of our school. Two of the police officers will remain with us to investigate this occurrence and will be asking questions of various students. If they select you to answer questions, I have no doubt that each and every one of you will cooperate to the best of your ability. And if any of you have information about this, the honor code requires you to reveal it. Given the duration of these alarms, please bear in mind that we will have to make up the instruction time on our first day of spring break, given the number of snow days we've already used up."

A chorus of loud groans and exclamations echoes through our class. Since Mom lost her job, our family couldn't afford to go anywhere for spring break anyway, but at least we were going to be out of school.

Ms. Robinson, who returned to the classroom during Mrs. J's announcement, sighs deeply. "Elizabeth, take your seat. You may join Andy in after school detention tomorrow afternoon."

Detention! I've never had it before. Maybe it will be just me and Andy. Maybe the detention teacher will get a call on her cell phone and have to step outside the classroom, or have to go down the hall to the copy machine. And Andy and I—the thought is interrupted as I get a mental glimpse of Mom's face. Geez, what am I thinking? I almost choke.

I can't go to detention. I've never gone to detention.

Ms. Robinson tries to change the visual on her SmartBoard, but no matter what key she presses, the screen shows the cartoon stork.

"Whoever is responsible for this," she says, "never fear, I have reported it to our IT administrator, Mr. Joya, and we will track you down." Then she turns on the light. "OK, people, let's read a chapter in our text instead of the visuals I had planned." She glances tiredly at Andy's empty desk, with his flour baby sitting there, wearing a backward blue baseball cap.

Andy's flour baby. A jolt races through me. Where's MY flour baby? Where is Ziggy? My mind scrambles as I check under and beside my desk. Did I leave her out on the soccer field? All by her lonesome? Is she just sitting out there, helpless on the grass, with the dampness and red North Carolina mud soaking through her thin paper skin? My own little Ziggy. I had set out to prove that I was responsible and wouldn't lose my flour baby and now, not only have I lost her twice, I've become a rebel like Andy and been sent to detention.

————

I run back to the soccer field before Biology to see if I can find Ziggy, but she is nowhere to be seen. Did someone pick her up? I don't have time to investigate or else I'll be late to class. When I skid through the door and stand beside Kelly, right at the bell, Mrs. Cruz is making an announcement.

"You have no idea how hard I fought for them to let me do this unit," she says. "I fought the administration as well as some parents. I thought it was absolutely necessary for you to have an actual dissection experience."

"Half our class isn't here," I say.

"Some students' parents insisted on taking them home after the fire drill today," says Mrs. Cruz. "And three students are meeting in the guidance office all week and viewing a Virtual Fetal Pig Dissection on the computer there because their parents don't think dissection is right." She turns on her SmartBoard to show us the segment of the video that we'll be dissecting today but instead of the video, on the screen is another cartoon drawing, this time of a chipmunk with long dark hair like Mrs. Cruz's.

Everybody starts to laugh, and Mrs. Cruz, after a gasp, quickly turns the SmartBoard off.

She turns to face the class and raises her voice. "Okay, people, before we get started, a word about these pranks. If any of you have any information about the person or persons doing this, please come forward. "

She stops and takes a breath. "Now, let's get started. Your goal today is to identify the heart, lungs, large intestine, small intestine, stomach, pancreas, liver, and kidneys. You may begin your work."

Dissection trays clatter onto the lab stations, the plastic crackles, and the formaldehyde, now free, assaults our noses in waves.

"So," Harrison says to me, "after palladium I'm going to get osmium. I bet you didn't know that it was first discovered in 1803."

"No, I didn't." Can't he tell that I'm only being polite?

He hangs over me like a vulture while I use the probe to pull the liver into view. It's one of the biggest organs, and dark. Breathing deeply and trying to ignore the seeping formaldehyde, I separate out the lungs. "Look how feathery they are. Kelly? Harrison? Do you want to do any cutting or probing?"

"I'll label the diagram," says Kelly.

"I'll make sure Lizzy's hair doesn't fall in her face." Harrison reaches over and, with one long gloved trembling finger, pushes a lock of my hair that's fallen out of my ponytail behind my ear. When his finger touches me, goose bumps race downward from the base of my skull. I shudder. "Harrison, stop!" I step away from the pig and glance over at Kelly.

As she looks up from labeling the lungs on her diagram, her eyes say, *Told you.*

Harrison hovers. I feel locked in an airless closet. "Piglet's looking a little worse for wear today," he says.

"Stop personifying our pig!" Kelly says. "And God, Harrison, Lizzy can't even breathe and I can't see. Could you move back?"

He steps back. He folds his arms across his narrow chest, and his eyes begin to burn with anger. I wonder if we've pushed him too far.

Carefully, I place the probe next to the heart. It is a small, dense fist of a thing, hard as a rock. In English class we sometimes use the word "soft-hearted," but looking at this heart, I cannot see how a heart can be soft and still keep a body alive. I think how hard the heart must work. It beats and beats and beats. It's responsible for everything. If it stops, life stops. The pressure to keep on going is always there, and it never lets up. I saw once on *Nova* that the human heart beats two and a half billion times in the average person's lifetime. It beats 100,000 times in one day. The heart works as hard all the time as your leg muscles work while you're sprinting.

We identify and describe the large and small intestines, then note the twin kidneys. Kelly says the pancreas looks like feta cheese. It does, sort of. I wipe the sweat from my temple with a gloved finger, trying to concentrate on what I'm learning and ignore the waves of nausea from the smell.

Right before the end of class, Mrs. Cruz reminds us what we're supposed to study before the dissection test on Friday. I check my phone and see that Andy has texted me three times. I was so caught up in the dissection I didn't even notice. On the way out the door, Kelly glances down the hall and sees Harrison standing there.

"Oh, no," she says, and ducks back inside, grabbing my wrist. "He's waiting for us."

I sigh. "Maybe you were right. Maybe he does like me."

"I know! Told you."

"What should we do?"

"Just don't look at him and walk really fast the other way."

We turn our faces toward one another to hide our laughing as we dart out of the classroom and away from him. I can feel him watching our backs as we scuttle away. I know we're being mean. I push away the feeling of guilt.

CHAPTER SIX

ON TUESDAY AFTERNOONS we have freshman cheerleading practice in the gym. The other ninth grade girls on the squad—the ones who haven't lost their flour babies—leave the babies on the bleachers while we spread out on the tumbling mats to stretch. Hopefully, since everybody is talking about the April Fools' pranks, no one will notice that Ziggy has gone *adios*, and I'll have time to get Ryan to take me to get another one this afternoon.

"Okay, so Mr. Waggoner's home page turned into a caricature of him as a badger and Ms. Robinson's turned into a stork," says Tanya, our cheer captain and our second-best tumbler after Marisa, as she slides her muscular dark legs into a split. Tanya is our undisputed leader. Leadership runs in her family; her mom was elected our first black head town councilwoman. And Tanya hasn't just got leadership potential; she also is extremely talented in art.

"Cody says that Mr. Murray's home page turned into a caricature of him as a slug," adds Marisa, dropping into an Olympic-caliber split, after I tell her about the caricature of Ms.

Cruz. "The police are interviewing suspects in that conference room behind the office. Since the alarm has gone off twice at the same time of day, they now think it's a computer hacker who set off the fire alarm system through the software that controls the building utilities. I saw Gordon, the kid from my bus who plays baseball, go in there. He's also in computer club."

He's also the one who's mean to Harrison, and who was tossing bags of flour yesterday with Brian.

"From a programming standpoint, those caricatures would not be hard to do," says Audrey, one of the bases in our formations, a strong girl with freckled skin and long, auburn hair. "I'm in computer club, and we talked about files like that— batch files that can open other files and then delete themselves. Harrison's in computer club, too. Maybe he did it." Audrey flattens her torso over her extended thigh.

"I know, he's definitely kind of weird," says Marisa. She gathers her thick, black hair into a tighter ponytail, then wipes sweat from her forehead with the back of her hand.

I almost stick up for him, say that my lab partner wouldn't do such a thing, but Marisa takes my hands to start a stretching exercise, and I say nothing. We sit on the mat with our legs in a V, the soles of our feet touching, and holding hands. We take turns lying back, pulling each other's arms, so that the other one's chest touches the mat. She's super flexible, so this exercise isn't a challenge for her, but I feel like she's dislocating both of my shoulders at the same time.

Now Tanya sits straight-legged with her toes pointed on the mat, and leans to touch her nose to her knees. "Well, there's also this kid in my art class who draws those anime cartoons all over his arms. You know, he calls himself Mr. X?"

"Oh, Lance Spock," I say, my voice strangled as Marisa pulls my arms to the breaking point. I smell rubber as my nose touches the mat. My hamstrings are on fire. The bones in my back could pop apart. "He definitely could have done the caricature that popped up on Ms. Robinson's screen as well as Mrs. Cruz's."

"If you knew who it was, would you tell?" I pull Marisa to a prone position.

"Rat them out?" she says, a bit squeaky, chest to cheek against the mat. "I don't know. Would you?"

I shrug. Then I think about Andy again. "Is Andy in computer club?" I ask Audrey.

"Of course he is," Audrey says. "What club is he not in? I don't know what I'd do. In computer club, we talk a lot about hacker morality, you know—white hats, gray hats, and black hats. There are a lot of hackers who just want to question the status quo. In their own way, they want to make the world a better place. There's a certain brilliance to that."

"But how is putting caricatures of teachers on the SmartBoard making the world a better place?" I ask.

"Well, maybe pointing out that there are holes in school security?" Audrey answers.

"I'd rat him out," says Tanya, her voice hard.

"How do you know it's a he?" I say.

"Oh, I don't know," she says. "I don't like him or her messing with us. We've already lost a freaking day of spring vacation!"

"You go, girl," says Marisa.

"Lizzy!" Miss Bebe, our cheerleading coach, is a tiny woman who used to be a flyer herself, with a big southern voice, big bleached blonde hair, and major league ambitions for us to win the state cheerleading championship in Raleigh next month. "Did you remember to bring a check from your parents for the competition? Everyone's brought theirs but you."

I slap my palm to my forehead and my face gets hot. "I'm sorry, Miss Bebe, I forgot again."

"You have *got* to bring it next practice. Otherwise you will not be allowed to compete."

"Yes, ma'am." Great. Something else I forgot.

"OK, ladies, let's get started!"

This year girls on our cheerleading squad have made more trips to the emergency room than the guys on the football team. Total, our squad has had seven sprained ankles, one broken leg, one broken elbow, three broken wrists, two broken noses, one concussion, one front tooth knocked out, and one slipped disc. I personally have sprained my right ankle twice and broken my tailbone once. The time I broke my tailbone, my family doctor and role model, Dr. Sharon Parker, told me to go to the grocery store, get a frozen bag of peas, and sit on them for twenty minutes three times a day.

She suggested I label them with permanent marker, "Elizabeth's Butt Peas" because you really don't want to eat peas that have served as "Butt Peas" as a previous job, even if they've been in a plastic bag.

OK, Dr. Parker actually called them "bottom" peas because Dr. Parker is super classy and went to Spelman College in Atlanta before going to Emory University for medical school, but I knew what she meant.

Dr. Parker is also Kelly's role model—a brilliant, black woman doctor who owns her own practice and is admired by everyone. Thinking about Dr. Parker, Kelly, and how Kelly and I have grown apart is making me kind of sad when I really need to be focusing on cheerleading practice.

When I tried out for cheerleading at the end of seventh grade, I didn't make it. When I saw my name wasn't posted on the door of the gym, I could feel myself falling into a deep, dark hole of despair. I didn't think I would be able to breathe another breath. Tears were trembling on my eyelids and I gritted my teeth to try and hold them back. I set my lips together and didn't think I could make a sound, but I managed to hug Marisa and Tanya and say, "Congratulations, I knew you'd make it." Wedged in the back of Marisa's mom's van with Marisa and Tanya, I rode home with my face frozen in a polite smile and a huge lump in my throat. I know Marisa and her mom tried not to act too excited about Marisa and Tanya making it, since I hadn't. My body felt like it was made of glass. I just tried to keep it from shattering.

I walked in our back door that night, and just seeing Ryan, Mom and Dad there watching the news together, I fell to pieces. Horrible raw sobs pushed up from the pit of my stomach. How could Marisa and Tanya have made it and I didn't? What did they have that I didn't have? Why wasn't I good enough? Ryan took one look at me and looked like he wanted to cry, too. Mom said, "Oh, Lizzy, you think it's the end of the world, but believe me, it's not." I didn't even try to explain to her the depth of my need to make the squad. Maybe I didn't even understand it completely myself. But somehow I wanted to belong in a way that didn't have anything to do with being the smart geeky girl who wants to be a doctor. I just wanted to be part of a team, to wear the uniform, to sing at the top of my lungs with everyone else on the bus.

Dad sat in his blue La-Z-Boy and took me in his arms and let me curl up there for almost an hour, crying until my head pounded and snot smeared my whole face. And then he said, very quietly into my ear, "You'll make it next year."

And for a year I took tumbling lessons and then came home and did handsprings in our front yard. Back-handspring-back-tucks in our back yard. Round-offs in our upstairs playroom. Marisa came over after practice and taught me how to make sharp movements with my arms during the dance routines. I don't know how many hours I practiced. Hundreds. Maybe thousands. But last year, I did make it.

And when I did, Dad patted me on the back and said, "Remember this when you're applying to medical school, Lizzy. How the hard work pays off."

Today we're working on standing back tucks. Miss Bebe wants every girl on the squad to be able to land one. "OK, ladies, line up!" She claps her hands. We count eight and do the tuck on five—leaping into the air and curling backwards into fetal balls. We try to land on our feet. But someone's knee always touches.

"Again! Until every single one of you lands it!" Miss Bebe knows just how many competition points will be deducted for a knee touching the floor, for a foot slipping outside the competition area, for an incorrect release, for a fall. She knows how many points we can earn with each perfectly executed back-handspring-back-tuck, each lay-out, each full, each double-up, double-down, scorpion, skater, or bow-and-arrow. The best choreographer in the state, she's always changing our routines at the last minute to rack up more points. She pushes us beyond what we think we can do, and she believes in us completely, and for that we all love her without reservation.

Again and again, we leap into the air, curl backward into fetal balls, and land on our feet.

"That looked like *crap*!" The word "crap" echoes through the metal struts at the top of the gym and ricochets back down. "Again! Now, stick it, ladies!"

One or two of us always wobbles, stumbles, falls to one knee.

After thirty minutes we are all winded and trembling and still we haven't succeeded. My body feels like a pillar of agony. I've landed every tuck so far but I know I only have one or two more in me. I close my eyes before each one, silently begging for the rest of the girls to do it right.

"Girls, if another squad came out here to watch y'all, they'd start laughing," Miss Bebe yells. "Again!"

But somehow, even when I think I can't do even one more, I do. By the time Ryan comes to pick me up I'm a sore, sweaty mass of frustration, and I feel about the size of a Butt Pea. But there's a sense of pride there, too. We did it. We went through the tough love of practice with Miss Bebe together, and we came out the other side.

"I have to go get another flour baby," I say to Ryan as I collapse into the front seat, my thighs twitching from lactic acid build-up, the bones of my shoulders feeling cracked and stretched, a hundred years old. How could adults possibly have more stress in their lives than I do?

"Kidding, you must be." Using Yoda's chirpy voice, Ryan checks the tension of my seat belt before putting the Camry in drive. He had a yearbook meeting after school and piles of notes slide across the back seat behind us.

"Well, with another prank fire drill, anyone could lose their flour baby." I pout.

"Yeah, this is crazy, isn't it?" He turns to stare at me before pulling away. "I heard they're interviewing suspects in the conference room behind the principal's office."

"They think it was the same kid who hacked the school computer. Marisa and Tanya think it's Harrison."

"Who's Harrison?" Ryan pulls out of the parking lot.

"He's one of my lab partners. We're dissecting a fetal pig." I hesitate. "He is kind of weird. He has a crush on me. He put my hair behind my ear so it wouldn't fall in the formaldehyde."

"No way!" Ryan exclaims, pretending to be outraged. "What a player!"

"But I don't like him, Ryan."

He parks in a space at the Harris Teeter across from the school. "A decent guy, he may be." His soulful brown eyes, eyes like Dad's, look tired as he hands me three soft wadded dollars. "You've got to stop losing these. I'm almost out of money. I'll wait here."

"You go, Ryan. Please?"

"This time, Lizzy, do it yourself you must."

I take a deep breath, and get out of the car, sliding the money into the elastic waistband of my cheerleading shorts. I head across the parking lot, looking back at him as he sits with the motor running, listening to the *Lord of the Rings* soundtrack. He waves at me and holds one thumb up.

I'm on the flour aisle, and have just grabbed a plump purple bag, when who do I see briskly crossing the back of the store? Ms. Robinson.

Oh no!

My mouth goes dry. Speed-walking to the other end of the aisle, I whip around the corner and stand with my back plastered against the bright plastic stacked containers of laundry detergent, like a criminal in a warehouse hiding from a cop.

I peek around the corner, and there is Ms. Robinson, heading down my aisle.

I hurry down another aisle and, while a lady has her back turned, I drop the telltale bag of flour into her cart. Before that lady sees me, I rush to the end of the aisle, and peek down to see where Ms. Robinson went. At the moment she turns the corner to head down my aisle, and I practically collide with her.

"Lizzy!" Ms. Robinson says. "Fancy meeting you here. Are you helping your mother shop?"

"Yes!" I say. But then she might want to talk to mom. "I mean, no! I—" *Thank God I ditched the flour.* "I just need..." I glance at the shelf next to me. "Cookie mix!" I reach out and grab a box, then clasp it next to my chest.

"Cookie mix?" Ms. Robinson cocks her head.

"Yes!" Sweat pops out under my arms. "Mom has a job

interview tomorrow and if she gets it I want to surprise her with cookies." This is not a lie. I *would* like to surprise Mom with cookies if she gets a job. That would make her happy with me, right? I just thought of it this instant. "So...I think I need some eggs too. Better run!"

Ms. Robinson gives me an odd smile. "That's kind of you, Lizzy. Not all students are so kind."

I think about the cartoon stork making fun of Ms. Robinson. I study her face. It never crossed my mind before, but could a teacher have hurt feelings?

"Ms. Robinson," I say, "you don't look like a stork."

She smiles. "I suppose there are worse things to look like. All right, then, see you tomorrow."

Throwing her an awkward smile, I race to the back of the store with the cookie mix and stand in front of the egg shelves, glancing back at her. I can't buy these two things because I don't have enough money. And we already have some at home. I have to ditch them and get out of the store without Ms. Robinson seeing me. Light streams in through the glass doors at the front of the store and they open with welcoming freedom. Before she can come down another aisle, I shove the cookie mix onto a shelf, and race back through the doors and out to the car, empty-handed and dizzy with fright.

"Ms. Robinson's in the store!" I jump in the Toyota, slam the door, and slide way down in my seat so I can't be seen through the window.

"The Health teacher? So?"

"We've got to go to another store, Ryan."

"You could be baking cookies and actually *need* flour."

I purse my lips and angle my eyes at him. "I tried that. Long story short, it didn't work."

Ryan is the best big brother in the world. After a long, patient sigh, he drives to the other store. I'm still so freaked that he even goes in and buys the flour for me again. By now he's getting into it. When he tosses the bag through the window at me, he says, "Say hello to Ziggy the Third. We've started a dynasty. You now owe me seven bucks."

As relief floods through me, I get out my permanent marker and go to work on Ziggy's face. I have it down pretty well by now. I thought the feeling of guilt would go away, but somehow it is twice as bad as when I got Ziggy Two. I push my hair out of my eyes, as if I could push the guilt away. I am going to come clean about this. This is only temporary—until I find Ziggy One. So I can get through the week without a zero in Health, and get Mom and Dad's permission to go to the dance.

I think.

———

"Does this look okay?" Mom asks when we walk in the house. "For my interview?" She twirls in black slacks and a long red jacket. The pattern of the v-neck underneath has red and black in it. "I already had the pants and jacket. I used a coupon and charged the v-neck."

"You look cool, Mom!" Ryan tells her.

"When's your interview again?"

"Lizzy! You're hopeless! Thursday at three-thirty!"

My stomach tightens. I am not hopeless. I *am* going to remember.

"I am so nervous," she goes on. "If it were a library job, I'd know what to talk about. With this, I have no idea. And let's face it: no one wants to hire anyone my age."

"I'd hire you," Ryan says, on his way upstairs.

"That's exactly what I'm afraid of." Mom points a finger at him. "A boss one third my age."

"We had another prank fire alarm," I say. "The principal

sent you an email. They think it might be a kid who's hacked the school computer."

"Really?" Mom says. "Wow, I hope they can track down who did it. They've been throwing the book at those hacker kids lately."

I think about what Audrey said today, about the hackers wanting to make the world a better place. I think about what she said about the white hats, the black hats, and the gray in between. When I was younger it seemed easy to tell the good guys from the bad guys. Now I am less sure. I start to say something, but instead just nod and head up the stairs.

———

After dinner, I'm sitting on my bed with a notebook open in front of me. Supposedly I'm doing my homework, but when I look down at the page I have doodled "Andy" in some sort of convoluted handwriting about twenty times. As Mom comes in my room with laundry, I quickly slide my textbook over the page. She examines Ziggy the Third, sitting on my dresser. "You've kept your flour baby so clean, Lizzy. I have to say I'm impressed. " She dumps unfolded laundry at the foot of my bed.

"See?" I say. "Maybe I'm more responsible than you thought." I look up at her and smile, but a painful lump forms halfway between my collarbone and my heart.

Mom narrows her eyes and leans closer to Ziggy. "The face looks different to me somehow. The mouth is ...I don't know... wider? And are the eyes closer together?"

"What are you talking about?" I carefully focus on my sheet of algebra problems. "How can it be different?" My mouth has gone a little dry.

Mom shrugs, and shoves the laundry aside. She sits on the end of my bed and stares at me. Then, she squeezes my toes through my socks. It feels really good. This is the nicest she's been to me since I forgot about her job interview. Is it possible she's forgiven me? "Remember when you went to that camp in the mountains for a week, when you were ten?"

"Yeah." There were zillions of bugs in the cabins. A mean girl stole my stash of M&M's. The swimming hole gave me an ear infection.

"I missed you so much." She squeezes my toes, looking off into the distance with watery eyes. A stripe of gray shows in her hair beside her part. The thought of her voluntarily doing this to save money makes me feel really upset, since it's basically my fault. "When I picked you up I got out of the car and saw all these kids in the main cabin standing beside their duffle bags. And even though it had only been a week, I barely recognized you." She looks back at me, eyes intense. "It wasn't just that you'd let some girl comb your hair straight up and dye the ends blue. It wasn't just that you seemed taller and thinner—I knew you'd hate the food. Your face actually looked different, as if the bone structure had changed. And your eyes had a brand new hardness and pain."

I start to tell her about the mean girl stealing my M&M's, but somehow I know she is saying something bigger than that.

"There was something in your face...you'd fended for yourself out in the big world for one week, and it had already changed you. And you were already moving away from me."

Tears prick my eyes. *I didn't want to move away from you*, I wanted to say. *You made me go to that camp!*

Mom gives my toes a last squeeze and stands up. "Anyway. Then you hugged me and in one instant, you were my Lizzy again. Maybe that's the deal with your flour baby. The face just looks different, like yours did at the end of that week of camp."

She leaves my room, just like that. I still don't know if she's forgiven me, and, even if she has, if she finds out about Ziggy and detention tomorrow afternoon, all forgiveness will be erased.

I definitely have a pounding headache. On *Five Minute Med Consult* it says I could have a tension headache, a concussion, a migraine, or a brain tumor. Dr. Sharon Parker, my role model, tells me that generally in medicine we should look for horses, not zebras—ordinary ailments rather than exotic ones. But still, I *could* have a brain tumor. It's possible.

I take a deep breath. On the plus side, even if I have to go to detention tomorrow, at least I'll get to see Andy. Is he worth being on the wrong side of Mom? As much as I hate to admit it, my case of AMSD is so bad that I would say "yes."

I wipe my face with my sleeve and try to get the lines of my math problem to straighten themselves out.

CHAPTER SEVEN

WEDNESDAY

THE BUS STOPS, and Harrison gets on. As he's sitting down behind Kelly and me, he says "Hey, cut it out!" We turn around. Gordon, behind him, snorting with laughter, has pulled up the waistband of Harrison's pants to give him a wedgie.

"Gordon! Cut it out!" I yell at him.

"Ha, ha, you're in love with Harrison!" Gordon taunts.

"No, I'm not. How can you say that?" I blurt out. Then I notice Harrison slumped in the seat behind us and I realize I've hurt his feelings. After a confused second, during which I think about Dad's advice and begin to doubt what I should have done or should do, I continue our conversation. "Marie Curie won the Nobel Prize twice, right?" I'd been embarrassed that I hadn't known who she was and looked her up in that biography Mom was reading.

"Right." Kelly turns on the little flashlight inside the test tube. "She wrote that the test tubes of radium glowed at night in her lab like fairy lights."

"That's cool."

"She and her husband Pierre were madly in love and they worked together in the lab into the wee hours of the night, amongst all those radium fairy lights."

"Wow." That sounds romantic to me. I think of being with Andy one night, surrounded by fairy lights.

Harrison leans between us. His breath smells sour. "From fairy lights to Fat Man and Little Boy."

"Fat Man and Little Boy?" I ask. Kelly pokes me, reminding me that I am supposed to ignore him.

"Robert Oppenheimer used Marie Curie's discovery to create the first nuclear bombs, Fat Man and Little Boy. Plus, Marie Curie died of exposure to radium, from carrying the radium test tubes in her pockets."

"Stop eavesdropping on all our conversations, Harrison," Kelly says. I wish she hadn't said that. But he is breathing on my hair and I feel like bugs are crawling on me.

"Why do you keep ignoring me?" Harrison blurts.

We don't turn to look at him, but I feel the heat of shame creep up my cheeks. "We're not," I lie.

"Yes, you are. You're pretending that I don't exist. Well, just wait. Maybe one day you'll know how it feels." Harrison slams out of his seat and moves across the bus aisle to another, glaring at us. We wait for the bus driver to yell at him but she doesn't notice.

Kelly and I cut our eyes at each other.

"Maybe we should apologize," I whisper.

"What for?" Kelly whispers back. "He can't force us to hang out with him." She hands a piece of gum across the aisle. "Here, Harrison. Here's some gum. But we're not best friends, all right?"

Harrison takes the gum. "Thanks, Kelly. It's cool you know so much about Marie Curie."

She nods, then sits back next to me.

I look at my lap, considering Dad's advice to be nice to everyone. Is Kelly right? I realize I don't know how to be nice to someone and not be friends.

As we are getting off the bus and walking into the school, Gordon steps on the heel of Harrison's shoe, making him stumble.

I step aside and walk by, leaving Harrison behind us.

————

Today on *The WLHS Show*, Andy interviews Tanya. Everyone on the squad knows Tanya is as tough as a tiger, but she has a sweet face and fools a lot of people. She has painted every possible surface of her flour baby with brilliant color. The front features one large eye and nose in black and white that appear to be from both front and side view at the same time.

"Wow!" Andy says. "So, Tanya, what did you name it?"

"Woman." Tanya has won a bunch of blue ribbons at art shows.

"It looks like we're seeing your flour baby's face from two different angles at the same time."

"That's cubism," Tanya says. "I did it to represent two different views of a woman—woman the parent and woman the artist."

Once Tanya stayed at her church for sixteen hours straight, painting a mural of the story of Jesus and the loaves and fishes in the hallway outside the Sunday school rooms. She hadn't stopped to eat, so her mother sent the other cheerleaders over with food and strict orders to make her stop and take a break. She sent enough food for the entire squad. Tanya's mural is amazing, with a dark-skinned Jesus preaching under a gigantic branching, twisty fig tree that looks hundreds of feet high. She used a magical-looking type of cubism to show the way the loaves and fishes multiplied to feed all of the people who came to listen.

Andy says, "Which is more important, Tanya, parenthood or art?"

Tanya knits her brows. "Why do I have to choose?"

"It's just hypothetical. Art or parenthood. Which?" Andy points his index finger at her.

"Get your finger out of my face, Andy Masters. I think you'd interview my grandmother on her deathbed and ask her what it feels like to die."

"So?" says Andy. "You've got to admit we all want to know." He grins and turns to the camera. "Til tomorrow this is Andy Masters." He knocks on his own head three times. "Mastering reality one day at a time."

Disapprovingly, Tanya purses her lips, and it gives me pause. All this time I've thought Andy was so funny and cool, yet here is someone I respect from the cheerleading squad who doesn't.

Marisa and I are leaving the cafeteria after lunch, with our flour babies in our arms, when Carly Lopez accidentally drops her lunch tray by the trash cans. The dishes and utensils clatter to the floor, and Marisa and a few other girls scream. I bobble Ziggy but manage not to drop her.

"Oh, my gosh, everyone is on edge," Marisa says.

"At least there's been no fake fire drill today," I point out.

We walk by the conference room beside the principal's office.

"See who comes out." Marisa slows her steps. "Wonder who they're interviewing now? Cody told me they interviewed Andy."

I widen my eyes. "Really? Why would they suspect him? Because he's in the computer club?"

Marisa nods. We can hear voices inside the conference room, but no one comes out, and we can't hang around the conference room door any longer without drawing attention, so we meander on.

"I'm dreading Biology," I tell her.

"Why?"

"My lab partner, Harrison. He has a crush on me."

"Oh, weird Harrison?"

I pause at *weird*, but still answer, "Yeah."

"Sorry. That sucks." Outside Biology Marisa grabs her nose. "Your classroom smells horrible!"

"It's the formaldehyde for dissecting the fetal pigs."

"I can't believe you can even do that."

"I have to, if I want to be a doctor. I kind of like it, to be honest."

Just then Harrison brushes past us into the classroom, giving me a dirty look.

"He doesn't act like he has a crush on you," Marisa whispers. "On the contrary."

"He's mad because Kelly and I ignored him on the bus."

"Oh." Marisa considers. "Well, if a person you don't like has a crush on you, you don't want to give them the wrong signals. But you shouldn't be mean, right?" Marisa heads down the hall. "Later."

Is she right about that? I mean, there's being mean. There's ignoring. And there's being nice, like Dad says. Be nice to everyone. Should I, then, be nicer to Harrison? Why do these things seem so simple to everybody else and so complicated to me?

Once in the classroom, I decide to be distantly polite to Harrison as he takes notes on the dissection. We work on the respiratory system today, identifying the nares (or nostrils), the glottis, the trachea, the bronchi, the bronchioles, and the alveoli.

The silence between us is tense and angry, but I answer politely. It doesn't seem to make a difference. He doesn't wait for Kelly and me to walk out of class this time; in fact, he just gives us a stern look and rushes out. It's just after that, when I turn to grab my backpack, that I realize Ziggy is gone again.

"Kelly, have you seen Ziggy?"

Kelly shakes her head, as she gathers her own things. "Did you have her when you got to class?"

"I'm almost sure I did!" I remember the bobble in the cafeteria for sure. "Oh my gosh! This is not happening. Where did I leave her?"

I just can't be this forgetful.

———

At the end of the day, after sprinting through the halls checking every classroom, searching for Ziggy the Third without success, I'm stuck in detention. Andy has not yet arrived. A wall of lockers lines this classroom and it smells like bologna sandwiches have been marinating in used athletic socks for at least two days. Carrie Raznik's Freddy Krueger flour baby leers at me with his staple teeth from the top of her desk. Lance Spock redraws a gigantic dragon on his forearm with a fine point marker. Brian Williams, the beefy football player who had the flour fight with Gordon during our first fire drill, runs his hands over his face but peeks at me between two of his fingers, smiling. I pull down the hem of my cheerleading skirt, trying to get it over my knees, but of course it's too short. I do not smile back.

The detention monitor is Ms. Stokel, a white woman with sallow skin who is built like a wrestler and seems to be only a few years older than me. "Shut your holes!" she shouts, even though we're not saying anything. She turns and writes on the board *Be quite! Q-U-I-T-E.* She turns back around, after proudly underlining her QUITE, and glares at us with narrowed eyes. "You may think you're gettin' away with murder in here but I have eyes in the back of my head!"

"So that's what those are," says Brian, a smile playing around his mouth.

"I said shut it!" Ms. Stokel curls her lip and points a pudgy finger at him. He goes silent.

Apparently, even though we're supposed to be "quite," the same requirements do not apply to Ms. Stokel. Her cell phone rings and she talks (complains) to someone while we, her prisoners, listen. I am normally not so rude as to eavesdrop on other people's cell phone conversations, but what choice do I have?

"Hey," she grunts into the phone. "I'm stuck in here with the usual bunch. Yeah. I can't believe they only pay me eight dollars an hour with no overtime and no dental plan. And no mental health! This job is enough to drive anybody stark raving mad, you know what I'm saying? Right."

I have a horrible sinking feeling. Will this go on for the entire time? When will Andy be here? Note to self: Do not be so foolish as to end up in detention ever again.

Finally she throws down her cell phone, puts her feet on the desk and starts clipping her fingernails.

How can I find out if Andy is on the detention list? I don't want to ask her because maybe he got out of it somehow.

I raise my hand. "Excuse me, I need to sharpen my pencil."

She glares at me with her slightly bulging eyes. "Just behind my desk."

I pick up my pencil and head past her chair. I vigorously sharpen my pencil, all the while craning my neck to see the names on the list. Then I see his name—and a scribbled note —"Baseball practice."

Realization spreads through my brain like a wildfire. I am in detention because of Andy and he's not even going to be here! He got out of it for freaking baseball practice! She starts talking and I barely hear what she says, I'm so sunk in disappointment.

"Are you going to sharpen that pencil to a nub?" she demands, more loudly.

"Oh, sorry." I take the pencil out of the sharpener and trudge back to my seat.

"So," she says, fixing us with a stare. "I bet it was one of you, wadn't it? " She gives a phlegmy laugh; she's tickled herself to no end. "Lance, it coulda been you in a heartbeat, huh? You probably play those video games and know the insides of a computer like the back of your hand. Not to mention those cartoons of yours."

Lance pulls his ski hat down over his ears and tightens his lips. He bears down harder on one of the dragon's fiery nostrils with the fine-tip marker but gives no other evidence he heard what she said.

My mouth hangs open. How can she say that? How can she accuse him, with no evidence at all? Aren't people innocent until proven guilty? Apparently not if you're under eighteen.

"Or you, Mr. Football Player. You think you can get away with anything, don't you? The rules don't apply to you, do they?"

Brian ignores her. Instead he slides his foot over and jostles Lance's leg, making him squiggle the marker and leave a lump on one of the dragon's nostrils. Lance glares at Brian with loathing, then licks a finger and tries to fix the ruined line, but the marker is permanent. So he puts a lump on the other side, creating symmetry.

Brian groans with boredom, and stretches his legs out in front of him. He crosses his arms over his chest and closes his eyes.

"Oh maybe it was you, Miss Raznik. Miss Radical Raznik. You with your Halloween-every-day-of-the-year fashion statements. Are you in the computer club?"

"Yes." Carrie speaks but does not otherwise react. She starts putting on black fingernail polish and the searing smell explodes inside my nostrils, making my eyes water. And I notice that Carrie's hands are shaking.

"Put away that nail polish this minute, Miss Raznik."

Very slowly, without expression, Carrie puts the polish away.

I did think Carrie was strangely over-competitive, maybe a bit subversive, but it never occurred to me that she could have hacked the school computer. And while we were evacuating, I did sort of wonder about Lance. But now, I would eat a bug rather than be like Ms. Stokel in any way. Just thinking about Carrie's shaking hands, I feel loyal to every kid in this classroom in a way I never have before.

So I make a stand. I say, "Hey, that's not fair." It comes out sounding like the soft cheeping of a baby chick.

"What's that?" Ms. Stokel swipes clipped fingernails, like chopped and discarded new moons, from the desk into the trashcan.

"I said that's not fair," I make my voice a bit louder. Just a little bit.

Carrie fixes me with a stare. Is it of gratitude? Or is it of disbelief that I've been so stupid as to let this woman get a rise out of me?

"Fair!" says Ms. Stokel. "I'll tell you what's not fair. It's not fair that SOME people can get straight As and do little flips and *pretend* to be sweet as sugar. No one would ever suspect you, would they, little Miss Lizzy? We're so glad to have you as our guest in detention today, Miss Lizzy. Lizzy Borden, maybe?"

Heat spreads over my face, slips up over my cheekbones and shoots around the tips of my ears. I know since I've had this crush on Andy it's like I've morphed into this totally different person, and I've forgotten a lot of stuff and done handsprings on the soccer field during a school evacuation and gotten a few extra flour babies. But Lizzy Borden killed her parents! Although, maybe it will kill my parents when they find out everything I've done this week.

But how can she judge me like that? I'm filled with fury, and then it turns into something else. I realize that up until this afternoon I've been judging everyone in this room.

———

After detention, Carrie and I are sitting on the curb outside the school waiting for our rides. She finishes putting on her black nail polish and offers me some.

"Sure," I say, pleasantly surprised, holding out my hand with my fingers spread. "I've never been in detention before, have you?"

She shakes her head as she smooths black nail polish on my thumbnail. "No. I thought your tumbling passes during the fire drill were awesome. Couldn't believe you did it. Thanks for standing up for us today, by the way."

"Hey, thanks. Why did you get sent to detention? "

"I corrected my history teacher. She got a date wrong."

"You're kidding!"

She shakes her head. "She thought I was being a smart aleck." She finishes the polish and blows gently on my fingertips to dry them.

"I have almost straight As," I say. "But I'm afraid I'm going to flunk Health. It seems so stupid."

"I'm afraid I'm going to flunk history because this teacher doesn't like me. She accused me of plagiarizing my history paper. She said it was too good. And she gave me a C minus."

"That is not fair!"

"I know," Carrie says. "I pay for being competitive."

CHAPTER EIGHT

"LIZZY, WHAT WERE YOU THINKING?" Ryan's eyes go wide with disbelief as I shuffle wearily toward the Camry. Late afternoon shadows stretch across the empty parking lot. The flag lines slap against the bare flagpole in the breeze. Carrie's mom picked her up ten minutes ago and I am the last one sitting here.

"God, Lizzy!" Ryan is so upset he jumps out of the car and smacks his forehead. "Like *The Invasion of the Body Snatchers*, this is. This morning you went to school as my dear, only slightly irresponsible, good citizen sister Lizzy. This afternoon, who do I pick up? A pod person! A juvie who hangs out in detention, you are!" He glares at my hands. "And paints her fingernails black!"

Bonding with Carrie had been unexpected. I shrug. "It was something to do."

At that moment, he glances over at the car next to us. All the tires are missing. "April Fools'?"

"Yeah. That's Mr. Waggoner's car. The comic book club did it, I think." Suddenly I wonder: The comic book club. Could the person who did the hacking on Ms. Robinson's computer be in the comic book club?

Ryan is so mad about detention, I don't even know if I have the guts to mention the loss of Ziggy. But I realize I have to. "Ryan, you have to understand, this has been the worst day ever."

"Obviously THAT goes without saying. I lived through it too. The cops are all over interviewing people."

"Right, even Andy! And everyone is nervous and twitchy, you know. And Harrison was mad at Kelly and me for ignoring him this morning, and he was mean to us in Biology. There was a lot going on, and detention was sooo horrible, Ryan, honestly, you have to believe me, it's not my fault." I toss my backpack in the back seat and wrench open the passenger door.

He is back in the car, starting the engine.

Suddenly he cuts his eyes back at me, realizing what I said. "What's not your fault?" He glances at my backpack. "Where's Ziggy?"

"Why do you keep nagging me about Ziggy?" I shout. "Can't you leave me alone about it? You're as bad as Mom and Dad!"

"Hey!" Ryan says. "What's going on with you?"

"You are not the boss of me! Just leave me alone!"

Ryan goes silent.

I immediately feel bad about my outburst. "Ryan, have a heart! I am doing the best I can!" I start to cry.

"You didn't, really, did you?" he says, his voice softer now. "Again?"

"Ryan, you have to help me!" I shut the car door, starting to wail. I hadn't realized how horrible detention was until I got out of there.

"Lizzy, how can I help you? I can't be inside your brain and remind you to remember stuff. You have to do it yourself."

I lose myself in crying. It's coming in a flood now and I can't stop. For some reason I think about that gray stripe in Mom's hair and how disappointed she is going to be with me. I love and feel so grateful to Ryan, and I see how hard he is trying to help me.

"Seatbelt, Lizzy," he says, with a deep, sad sigh. He pulls out of the lot.

I keep crying for a few more minutes, thinking about what a failure I've been this week and how I've let myself and everyone in my family down. My throat aches and my eyes throb. When I realize that Ryan is indeed turning into the grocery store parking lot, fresh tears spring from my eyes and my feelings of guilt double.

Here he is, trying to help me and I am just a worthless forgetful ninny. Why am I like this? And now it's even worse because of Andy.

———

"All right, Lizzy," he says. "Do your thing." He pulls out his wallet and opens it and I can see that I am taking his last three dollars. "This has got to be it. I'm completely broke after this."

"I can't take the last of your money." I wipe my wet cheeks. I feel like I'm about to sink through the floor of the car.

"Why not?" He gives me a sharp look.

"I'll pay for it myself!"

"Right." Ryan cocks his head. He knows I'm broke. I'm counting the days until I babysit for Casey because it will be my first money in several weeks.

"Just take it, Lizzy."

I take his money and slink across the parking lot. Once inside, I shuffle to the baking aisle and grab another bag of flour. So much for being able to prove anything about myself to anyone. Mom and Ryan are right, I'm hopeless. I pay for the flour and skulk back to the car.

"Ziggy the Fourth." I toss the bag of flour onto the floor, give Ryan the change, and shut the car door. "Ziggy Stardust. Like that David Bowie album Mom used to play."

Ryan is silent as he pulls out of the parking lot.

"I promise, this is the last one," I tell him. "I've changed. I'm going to be responsible now."

Ryan gives me a deeply skeptical look. "Lizzy, you're on a downward spiral and you've hit a new low. What is going on with you?"

We drive in uncomfortable silence for a few minutes. "I guess I have been distracted. If a guy invites a girl to a dance, does that mean he expects her to...fool around?"

"If you're talking about that roving reporter, the guy who called you his little pomme frite, my guess is 'yes,' probably."

"You don't even know him, Ryan!"

"I know his type."

"No you don't. He's not a 'type.' He's a person, an individual person. A very funny and charming person, for your information. One of the most popular guys in the whole ninth grade." Why did I ever ask Ryan about this, anyway?

"Don't say the word 'popular' in my presence, I beg you. "

"And he happens to like me. Is it so unbelievable that somebody might like me?"

Ryan grimaces. "No. Even before you became a juvenile delinquent, you were a very appealing person, believe it or not."

"I'm not a juvenile delinquent!"

"It was an expression. Anyway, whether a guy finds you attractive is not what we were talking about. You asked me if I thought he was hoping to fool around if he invited you to a party. An honest answer I gave you: Yes."

I stare out the window at the stone wall that frames the

entrance to our neighborhood as Ryan turns down our driveway. "Well, what if I went to the party, and I just said no?"

Ryan glances at me and shrugs. "Within your rights, that certainly is. It's just that, Lizzy, it takes a while to really get to know a person. Just like, someone looking at you now might think you're a shallow cheerleader type, but you're not."

"Why does everybody think cheerleaders are shallow?" I snap.

I feel so frustrated by the conversation that when getting out of the car I accidentally slam the shoulder strap of my backpack in the car door.

"I hate this backpack! I hate this car!" With bottled-up rage, I wrench it out and we walk through the garage without speaking. I remember Mom texted saying she went to a seminar about successful job interviews and will be late.

When we get inside Ryan hits the button on the phone to play back any messages and there is the voice of none other than Mrs. J on our answering machine telling Mom and Dad that I have detention this afternoon.

"Oh, no!" I say. "This is like my worst nightmare!" I start to cry. "Please, just delete it."

"You have to tell them, Lizzy," Ryan says.

"I will. I will tell them. But it will be so much better if they find out from me than from Mrs. J on the answering machine."

He hits the delete button. "Tell them, or I will."

I feel like hugging Ryan. "Okay, I will. I'll tell them tonight."

"Sounds good," he says. A half hour later, Ryan leaves to go to work at the car wash, and I am home alone.

I take my time decorating the fourth incarnation of Ziggy with the marker I've been carrying in my purse. I forge Ms. Robinson's signature on the bottom as usual, and give myself a pep talk. Maybe this flour baby will take. Maybe this will be the permanent one, the one I will keep forever. Or at least until the end of the week.

I promise myself that I will get my mind off of Andy. I'm mad at him anyway. I'm going to change. I'll prove to Mom and Dad and Ryan that I can be responsible after all.

I make her eyes look a bit like an ancient Egyptian painting. I figure, in the aftermath of two fire drills and a school computer hack, what teacher is going to notice that her eyes suddenly look a bit more dramatic than yesterday?

Andy, on his way home from baseball practice, texts me. It says,

Can't help it that I'm so popular.

After a few more seemingly random lines, I start laughing. He's typing in lines from movies. But wait. I'm supposed to be mad at him because he got me sent to detention and never showed up himself. I start to text him back and ask where he was, but then I decide I don't want to be a nag, so I just text back:

Mean Girls.

A minute or so later he sends me:

John Cusack holding a boom box.

I know that one too. At first you'd think it was "Say Anything," because that's the movie the scene's in, but the movie with the actual line of dialogue is:

Easy A, I text.

I hate your big dumb combat boots.

I text back: **10 Things I Hate About You**.

He texts, **Crushed it**.

I text back: **Pitch Perfect**.

He texts**, A watch doesn't go with this outfit**.

I text back: **Clueless**.

After ten minutes I've completely forgotten that I was

mad at him at all. That's the way Andy is. He starts sending more and I'm giggling and trying to keep up when the phone rings.

A formal male voice says, "Is Mrs. Ellen Winston there?"

"She's not here right now," I say. "May I please take a message?" Understanding washes over me: This is about a job. I can't mess up again. I hurry around the counter to the corner where Mom keeps pads and pencils, grasping the phone between my ear and my shoulder, dropping it, wedging it back, dropping the pencil, picking it up, holding it poised above the paper.

"Yes, one of the people I was planning to interview tomorrow canceled and I was wondering if she could come in an hour earlier, at two-thirty instead of three-thirty? Could you please give her that message? If she has questions she can call this number."

I scribble it all down.

"Thank you." The man hangs up.

I am starting to text Mom to tell her about it when Andy sends me another text message. **I AM Ironman.**

When Mom found out I'd forgotten to give her the message about the last job interview, she smashed a glass into the dishwasher hard enough to break it, then bent and piled the broken glass in the palm of her hand, stacking the curved broken pieces. She poked her thumb with a ragged edge, smearing the glass with streaks of blood, and still she kept picking up pieces, every now and then sticking her thumb in her mouth to staunch the blood flow.

I ran into the laundry room where we keep our first aid kit and brought her a limp gummy bandage. She leveled her dark eyes on me and it felt like thunderbolts came out of them. Dumping the stack of broken glass into the trash can, she grabbed the bandage, but then couldn't get the paper off without using her thumb. I took it back from her and peeled the ancient white backing.

"Here," I said. My mother held her thumb out for me and I wrapped a bandage around it as carefully as I could. "Sorry," I told her. "You don't need stitches."

"How do you know?" she yelled.

"Because I looked it up once. It has to be deep enough to expose fatty tissue, and it's not."

"This forgetfulness stuff used to be cute when you were little," she said, ignoring my reassurances. "But you're not little anymore and it's not cute anymore and it makes me think that you just don't care. In the future, Lizzy, if you're not going to be responsible enough to take a message, don't answer the phone. Let it go to voicemail."

Normally when she loses her temper and yells at me she apologizes later. But this time she never did. And I can't help but think that she hasn't forgiven me.

So now, I immediately text her the message, leaving the name and number of the person who called. This time, I'm not forgetting. I have changed.

A moment later, Dad comes in, laying his briefcase on the counter as usual. He kisses my forehead. "How was your day, sweetie?"

"Fine. Someone just called Mom about a job interview. They want her to come earlier."

Dad raises his eyebrows and smiles. "Excellent!" he says. Then he gets his laptop and a manila folder out of his briefcase. He pages through budget documents with columns of numbers on them. Then he goes over to the phone to play the messages. I break out in a cold sweat. "No messages," says the robotic voice.

I feel as limp as a noodle. I should tell Dad now about detention. But I can't make myself. I can't bear to see that disappointed look on his usually happy, ruddy face. I tell myself it will be better to tell Mom and Dad together, and I'll do it later. Maybe after Mom's interview.

"Yeah. I hope she gets the job," I say. I lean on the counter. Mom's not here. Ryan's not here. Maybe Dad will be supportive about Andy. "I have a question."

"Shoot." Dad shuts his laptop, sits at the counter and folds his hands over his stomach.

"There's this guy that likes me."

"Oh, there is, is there?" Dad smiles. "And how do you know that?"

"He messages me all the time. Sends me little jokes. He sent me a funny video from YouTube of two otters holding hands. And penguins walking along together."

Dad nods sagely. "Yep, he likes you. Do you like him?"

"I think so. I guess. I think about him a lot, about whether he notices me or what he thinks about me." I start to twirl a chunk of my hair, so nervous about asking the question. "The thing is... how did you know you were in love with Mom?"

"Oh, Lizzy, we were much older. It's totally different. You're too young to be in love. You have a crush."

"Romeo and Juliet were about my age."

"Yes, and look how that worked out," Dad says dryly.

I twirl my hair more tightly around my finger and watch as the tip of my finger turns red. "Well, I know, but how did you and Mom meet?"

He smiles. "I haven't thought about that in a long time. She and I met in a play in a community theatre."

"You and Mom used to act?" It's almost impossible to imagine. My super-responsible Dad and my tired, angry Mom.

"In our spare time, yes. She was a librarian by day and an actress by night. I was a non-profit administrator by day and an actor by night. We both had what you might call dual personalities. We were doing *The Importance of Being Earnest*. I played Jack and she played Gwendolyn."

"I don't know the story."

"The two are in love but they have obstacles. First, Gwendolyn's mother doesn't approve of Jack. Also Gwendolyn swore years ago only to marry a man named Ernest, and that's what she thinks Jack's name is. He's lied to her about his name so she'll marry him."

"That sounds ridiculous, Dad. Why would a person decide who to marry based on their name?"

"I know; I realized that just when I was telling it." He laughs and shakes his head. "But in the end it turns out he was lost by his nanny in a handbag, and was adopted and given the name of Jack by his adoptive parents. Guess what his real parents had named him?"

"Uh...Ernest?"

"Correct!" Dad looks off into space. His tired face takes on a tender expression.

"Sorry, Dad, it sounds really stupid."

"Yes...it's a type of play called a farce, so some of the things that happen are ridiculous. But it also gets you thinking, what are reasonable qualities for choosing another person? The other person doesn't have to be named Ernest, but that person definitely should have the *quality* of being earnest. "

"So while you were working on the play, you and Mom fell in love? Did you tell her that you loved her?"

"It's funny, my lines in the play called for me to tell her I loved her, so I told her every night in the play, but not in real life. In real life I hinted at it in many ways—by picking up an extra cup of coffee for her when I stopped on the way to the theatre, by saving her a seat when we had cast meetings, by touching her arm when I talked with her. But in actual words? Not for a long time. And then one night, during the performance, when I said my lines, she knew it was me speaking through the character. And at that point, there was not much she could have done or not done that would have made me stop loving her." Dad stares out the kitchen window at darkening sky. I feel like he is far away. Shadows spread through the kitchen. He gets up and flips the light switch, and the glare from the light seems to change the nature of our conversation. "But Lizzy," he adds, "you're only fifteen."

"Sixteen this summer."

"You have a long time before the time is right for you."

"Well, and his name isn't Ernest," I joke.

"That's right—so just forget him!" Dad laughs. "It's fine to have a crush." Dad hesitates, like he's trying to read between the lines. "Maybe you've heard people talking about this and you think you have to do it to hang onto your friends."

I think about my pact with Kelly. *Nope, just the opposite.* But Marisa and a lot of the other cheerleaders have boyfriends... so *am* I feeling that kind of pressure?

"Oh—and be like Gwendolyn. Don't spend your time with any young man who isn't earnest! Not the name, the quality of being earnest." Dad laughs at his own joke.

"What does earnest mean?"

"Look it up. Use my laptop." When he opens the laptop, I come around and look over his shoulder at the screen. Dad has a musty, office smell, a smell of a long day. He finds the online dictionary and types in "earnest."

earnest: *serious and intense; not joking or playful; zealous and sincere.*

OK, then. I believe the entire student body of Lakeside High would agree. Earnest. That is something that Andy definitely is not.

And I wish I'd never asked Dad about Andy.

Later, I am feeling pretty responsible because I don't text with Andy again until after my homework is done.

Text me your day in emojis, he says.

I start to laugh, then I send him a line of emojis—a school bus, a pencil, a desk, a little cheerleader, a car, a few food items, and a pencil again for homework. I am laughing the whole time. He sends me a line of emojis, too, which includes a baseball player and pizza.

Then he asks me again.

How are you, Liz my tiz? Did you decide about the freshman dance Friday night?

I try to imagine what being at the dance will be like. The Lakeside prom is usually at a hotel in downtown Charlotte, but the freshman dance is in the gym, with lots of chaperones. Punch bowls. Potato chips. Pretzels. I picture sitting next to him in a folding chair. Will we slow dance? I think about what Ryan said about Andy's hopes of fooling around, and about it taking a while to get to know a person. Then I remember what Kelly said, about it being April Fools' week. Could Andy have asked me to the dance as a prank? Why did she say that? Why did she put that in my mind? So, does he really like me?

I don't know, I finally tell him. **I ended up in detention today because of you and you weren't even there.**

Oh! Sorry. My coach got me out of it.

I found that out. Did you get the interview you were trying to get today about the computer hack?

Yeah, wait till you see it. Sometimes you need to ask the right people the right questions. It's going to be a blast.

I feel like he should thank me for my help with the tumbling distraction. But I don't bring that up. Instead, I type: **So what did you ask? And who?**

You'll see. Sometimes you need just need to know the right people.

A funny kind of pressure builds in my chest and I feel like I can't catch my breath. I remember the way Tanya seemed to disapprove of Andy. And that the cops interviewed Andy in the conference room. **What right people?**

You'll find out!

What does he mean by that? We kid around a little more but then I tell him I have to go. I barely allow the thought to form, but it insists on coming anyway: could Andy possibly have something to do with the computer hack? And what if he did ask me to the dance as a prank? Goosebumps creep slowly up the back of my neck.

CHAPTER NINE

THURSDAY

FOR SOME REASON, a lot of people don't sit in their assigned seats on the bus today, and Mrs. McCready doesn't even yell at them. But Kelly still slides into the seat next to me. Harrison sits behind us again and, because he seemed so mad yesterday, I give him a slight smile.

"So I heard they interviewed Andy about the pranks," Kelly says.

"He wouldn't do the pranks. He just wants to report on them," I say.

"How do you know?"

I shrug, getting irritated. "I just know."

"I don't see how you could know him all that well after just a five day text-fest." Kelly examines her cuticles.

"Well, I have been in class with him for three months." She must be jealous. That's all I can figure out. "Kelly, are you jealous that Andy and I are talking to each other?"

She throws her head back and laughs. "Jealous! That's the most ridiculous thing I ever heard."

"Well, I think so, too. But I'm trying to figure out why you're being like this."

Suddenly she's serious, like she's worried about me, and I feel those goosebumps on my neck again. "I just don't think he's the person you think he is."

Harrison suddenly thrusts his chin between us and says, in a vampire accent, "I vant to bite your neck! I vant to suck your blood!"

We both scream.

As we file off the bus, Gordon puts a sticky note on Harrison's backpack that says, "I pick my nose and eat it." Kelly grabs the note, balls it up, and throws it in the trash. Harrison never knew it was there.

When we get to school, cops are walking the halls. They aren't friendly; they glare at us like we're all guilty. I tense up. In homeroom, I scoot my chair closer to my desk as I watch *The WLHS Show*. Whatever is on the show today will be what I made possible yesterday with my tumbling. Guilt makes my muscles even tenser. I stare at the screen, watch a close-up of Andy following a female police officer with a microphone. The police officer turns to the camera, a deep frown crossing her serious face. "Young man, students are not allowed in the building at this time. You need to evacuate immediately."

"What have you found?" Andy says. "Can you tell us?"

"You need to evacuate, right now. How did you get in here? Do you think this is some kind of joke?" Her voice is stern.

"Do you have any leads?"

The police officer leans close to the camera, and her features look huge. "Do you realize that if there was a fire in here you could be DEAD? Out. Now." Her hand covers the camera lens.

The TV screen goes black.

Now we see Andy again, in a dark hallway beside an empty classroom, speaking into the microphone. "The police officer was not that cooperative, frankly. I am neither on the side of the administration nor of the students. I am an objective reporter, on the side of truth. All of us, students and administration alike, want to know who is pulling these pranks. One student has agreed to talk about it with us anonymously."

Andy now steps into the empty, darkened classroom, where a slumping, skinny guys sits in front of a window. He wears a Bugs Bunny face mask and when he shifts in his chair, I catch a quick glimpse of something on his forearm.

A drawing.

A dragon.

Oh, my gosh, it's Lance! I can't believe I've recognized him from his tattoo.

When he talks, Andy has altered Lance's voice so it's a high rapid Bronx accent, like Bugs Bunny. When we hear it, everyone in homeroom laughs nervously. But it also sounds kind of scary.

"Well, first they searched me and my backpack. They took out all the pens I use for my drawings and asked me about them," Lance crosses his arms over his chest; he's nervous. "Then they asked me where my classes were that day. They asked me if I was in computer club and if we'd ever talked about how to hack a computer. They asked me to take them to my locker, and then they searched it."

"Did they ask permission to search your locker?"

"No. They told me because I'm in school they don't have to ask permission."

"Did they find anything interesting?"

"Well, they took a long time looking at my drawings."

Someone in the classroom says "Silly wabbit!" and no one laughs.

"Did they ask you anything else?"

"They asked me if I knew of anyone who might have done it."

"If you did, would you tell?"

"I don't know," Lance says.

"Thanks for the interview."

"No problem," says Lance.

"Ba-dee, ba-dee, that's all, folks," Andy says, and steps back into the hall with his microphone. "The question is, what would you do? How many students at Lakeside High would turn in this person or people, if they knew? Remember, we've already lost one day of spring break. According to the honor code, turning each other in is what we're supposed to do. How many of us would follow the honor code in this situation? How many students at Lakeside High believe this is just a prank, and all we should do is laugh? How many people think the hackers are making an important point, which is that school computer systems are not very secure? Today I'm going to be coming around and asking people. Tell me what you think." He signs off.

Today, no one laughs when he knocks on his head. Andy has changed. The idea of him mastering reality one day at a time, which was funny yesterday, now seems serious. He's challenging us to take a position in this situation.

I watch Andy's eyes, burning with a new passion. Now the word "earnest" seems to fit him, when yesterday it didn't fit at all.

According to Dad, now that he's earnest, I can say "yes" about the dance. But I'm confused. Did Andy set up the fake fire drills to make some kind of journalistic point? He seems to be enjoying all of this way too much.

But I still want to say "yes."

Later, in Health class, Ms. Robinson gets us quiet, switches off the lights, and puts the color photo of the developing baby in the womb on the SmartBoard. Researchers have learned that the baby at thirty weeks can produce tears inside the womb. Then, without warning, the stork image fills the screen again. Mrs. Robinson jumps.

"I talked with Mr. Joya about this, and we've all changed our passwords. This shouldn't be happening." She sighs and turns her computer off.

The loudspeaker pops. "Andy Masters," comes Ms. J's terse voice. "Report to the office immediately."

Andy stands slowly. He bites his lip, and leaves the room.

Then, in the midst of the quiet, the fire bell shrieks.

Ms. Robinson stops speaking mid-sentence. "Not again." She turns on the lights. "Please file quietly out of the classroom and onto the soccer field."

It's too much of a coincidence that Andy has just been called to the office.

Chair legs squeal, people moan, books slam onto desks. In moments we are at the door.

Minutes later the cruiser arrives. Its blue light isn't even on today and the black and white sedan glides without an iota of fanfare onto the turnaround beside the school.

As usual, I left Ziggy in the classroom and my arms feel empty without her. Marisa and I sit side by side and I look for Andy.

"I wish we could go home," she says, repeatedly running her thick ponytail through her hands.

"Yeah. Wonder why Andy's not back from the principal's office."

Marisa glances at the school entrance and back at me. "Do you think they suspect him?"

"I don't know." I don't want to be suspicious of Andy. But he seems so energized by the investigation and so excited about the honor code issue. That whole interview with Lance was creepy.

"Why would they suspect him? Did he do anything?" Marisa persists.

I wrap my arms around my stomach. "I don't know, but I'm going to find out."

After about thirty minutes, the police and firefighters come back down the marble steps and slide heavily into the cars. My stomach cramps harder as I wonder if Andy's getting into trouble for what he did on the morning show. I wish I could talk to him.

Fleetingly, I wonder if I have appendicitis.

In record time the cruiser is gone.

"You may return to your classrooms at this time," booms Mrs. J's God-like voice.

————

Ziggy survived the third evacuation intact; she sits on my desk when I return. I cradle my little baby with her lovely Egyptian eyes in my arms. I have made it through the fire drill without losing her. Miraculously.

Andy's seat is empty.

My breath catches in my throat. Something is wrong. I know it.

In our darkened classroom, Ms. Robinson again begins droning on about the floating fetus. I put my head on my desk, to tune her out, and my cell phone vibrates. Very stealthily, I hold it inside my desk to read the text. Andy. My face heats up.

I'm suspended.

I gulp. **Y**?

For going back into the school for the cop interview. Favor?

What?

HUGE secret. After school, come get the memory card of new interview I will be doing today about fire drill pranks and take it to Billy Z for the show tomorrow. Please?

Who is the interview with?

Can't tell you. Plz.

Why can't he tell me?

If I help Andy, will I get in trouble? If I go by his house this afternoon, and he's somehow involved, I might find out. Is it possible he would stage the fire drills to make a more exciting *The WLHS Show*?

I take a deep breath. What if I see something? Then I'll know for sure. Then I'll have to decide whether to tell or not.

But what if Andy makes me swear not to tell?

I start to text Andy back, saying "OK," but suddenly someone is leaning over me.

"Your phone, please, Lizzy." Ms. Robinson holds out her hand.

Caught! I gulp and hand it over. I feel like I've lost my arm.

"You'll get it back at the end of the day."

———

Kelly, Harrison, and I gather around the lab station in Biology. Mrs. Cruz gives us instructions to identify the abdominal aorta, the renal artery, the carotid artery, the femoral artery, the internal iliac artery, the umbilical artery, and the spleen.

I try to concentrate, Andy's favor keeps rolling round and round in my head. I have no way of texting him back. My fingers fumble as I try to separate the blood vessels without severing them.

Pale and quiet, Harrison looks at Kelly, and especially at me, with a seething glitter in his eyes. His temples seem particularly bony. I think about Gordon putting that sticky note on his backpack today, and I feel bad for him. I'm glad that Kelly threw it away. Since being in detention, I guess I am more aware of judging others harshly, and I don't want to be like that.

Kelly leaves to go to the bathroom, and after working with Harrison in uncomfortable silence for a few minutes, I ask him, "So, how long have you been collecting the periodic elements?"

"Since I was in fifth grade."

"Why did you decide to do that, as opposed to collecting stamps or something like that?"

"For your information, these elements are everything there is in the universe," he says, then adds, after a hesitation, "Are you making fun of me?"

"No! Why would you say that?" Heat rises to my face.

"Because a fair amount of time people are making fun of me," he says. "It hasn't escaped my notice." A blood vessel pumps in his temple.

So he knows how people feel about him. I guess I knew that all along, even though he pretended to ignore everything. I fumble around for another question. "So, I guess you're going to collect them all, huh?"

He snorts. "Obviously not. Mercury is poisonous, for your information. Also, some elements are radioactive. I'm obviously not going to collect them."

"Oh, right."

"And some elements only exist for a few nanoseconds

before breaking down. How would you suggest that I collect them?"

Now he sounds like he's making fun of me. Why is it so hard to have an ordinary conversation with him?

"Obviously," he goes on, "anyone with a brain could figure out that I'm only collecting those elements that naturally occur in nature."

Okay, so now he's accusing me of not having a brain. My eyes throb with anger and, slashing with the probe, I accidentally cut a blood vessel in two. I wish I'd never talked to him!

At that moment, to my great relief, Kelly comes back. I concentrate and poke at Piglet's spleen. "You can live without a spleen," I say.

"Right." Kelly nods.

Harrison says, "Have you ever eaten chicken livers? What about Piglet spleens?"

"Harrison, gross!" Kelly and I both yell at the same time.

"What seems to be the problem, ladies?" Mrs. Cruz is suddenly beside us, her hands on her hips, studying first Harrison's face, then Kelly's, then mine. Kelly shoots me a look and neither of us answer.

"Nothing," I say. "Typical boy stuff, grossing us out." I give Mrs. Cruz an exasperated smile.

Mrs. Cruz studies us for what seems like an eternity. She is not a teacher who ever falls for anything. "All right, then get back to work," she finally says, tossing her glossy dark hair. She moves away.

Heaving a sigh of relief, I carefully separate the aorta, then the carotid artery. They seem like flimsy blue rubber bands. I know that the blue isn't blood but dye.

I toss hair out of my eyes and Harrison moves his whitish

rubber-gloved hand to push it back for me. He stops when I flinch, and lets his hand drop like a falling bird.

Even though I'm looking at Piglet, and not at Harrison, I can feel the sadness flowing from him like fog. Exhaling hard, I focus on separating the arteries I feel like there is suddenly much more going on here than I realized before, and I don't know what to do about it.

CHAPTER TEN

MARISA, Tanya, and I take turns slurping from the water fountain in the hall outside the gym. I wipe sweat from my temples with the backs of my hands. Miss Bebe made us run twenty laps and do a hundred sit-ups before practice even started. She's in a "you girls look like crap" mood, but at least she gave us a water break. I'm still out of breath and sweat tickles as it rolls down between my boobs. My stomach muscles quiver.

I got my phone back, with a lecture from Ms. Robinson, but it was dead so I still can't text Andy back.

"Just tell me who that sucker is, and I'll burn his ass," Tanya says. "I'll get him back for making me stand outside in the humidity today and making my hair curl." She readjusts her dark ponytail, smoothing the hair more tightly over her head.

I keep my mouth shut about Andy, waiting to see if any of the cheerleaders know he's been suspended.

"The cops interviewed Cody today," Marisa says.

"They interviewed Cody?" I cock my head in disbelief. Cody makes straight As and is on the Odyssey of the Mind team.

"Cody?" Tanya repeats. "He's like the Upstanding Citizen poster boy."

"I know, right?" says Marisa. "I guess they're interviewing everyone who even has a class in computers or video games. Cody tried to ask them if they had any leads but they wouldn't tell him a thing."

At the end of practice Miss Bebe calls us to gather around and we sit cross-legged in a tight semicircle. It's hot in the gym and our sweaty legs stick to the mat. She steps up onto the first row of bleachers and claps her hands. "Now listen up, girls," she says. "I just want to make something perfectly clear. If any one of you has even the tiniest bit of information about who's doing this, let me tell you, this is no joke. I expect each and every girl on my cheer squad to do her civic duty and turn in any and all information you may have. This is your obligation as a good citizen. It's what is required by this school's honor code."

She puts her arm in the air. "Raise your hand to let me know you understand what I have just said to you."

We raise our hands in silence. I have a terrible headache, all of a sudden.

"All right, then. You girls may go."

As we're walking out of the gym, Miss Bebe says to me, "Lizzy, did you bring your permission slip?"

Guilt sweeps across the skin of my scalp like an electrical circuit. "I can bring it tomorrow," I say as quickly as I can. I can't believe I forgot it *again*.

"No, it was due days ago, Lizzy. That's it, You're out of the routine. You won't be able to go to the competition next weekend."

Marisa is standing next to me and she gasps. I feel like I'm dropping through a hole in the floor.

"Miss Bebe, I can get it this afternoon—"

"Nope. That was your last chance, Lizzy. No need for you to come to practice for the rest of the week."

I head out of the gym, tears rolling down my cheeks. My feet feel like lead weights. I can't believe this. I'm missing the competition. What I live for!

In the parking lot Marisa catches up with me. "Lizzy, wait up," she says. "I'm so sorry, I can't believe she did that. I never thought she would."

My nose begins to run and my throat starts to hurt. "Me either! What am I going to do?" It's all I can do to keep from breaking down and sobbing. Marisa gives me a long hug.

She waves to Ryan as the Camry glides up. "Call or text me later if you need to."

———

After Marisa leaves, I don't want Ryan to know about the forgotten permission slip, so I quickly wipe away the tears and pretend to be cheerful. I hold Ziggy IV aloft to show him, as if presenting her to throngs of adoring subjects. "We don't have to go to the grocery store, can you believe it?" As he pulls out of the parking lot and I slide down in the front seat, he glances at me a few times and I wonder if my eyes are red or something.

"Have you been crying?"

"No. Allergies, I guess." To further convince him, I take off my cheerleading shoes, and put my bare feet out the window. I can't tell Ryan about the competition. He'll just say "I told you so." But what's now on my mind is whether I'm going to do what Andy asked and go by his house to get the memory card for that interview.

"I don't need to smell your feet," Ryan says.

The air still feels damp from a light rain earlier today but the sun is out and drying raindrops sparkle on the cars' hoods and windshields. I wiggle my toes so the breeze scoots between them.

Ryan glances at me again. "Is something wrong?"

"No." I turn my face away and pull my feet in.

We pass the post office and I know we'll be coming up to the turn to Andy's house any minute. "Hey," I say. "My friend Andy missed health class today and I have to lend him my book. Can you drive by his house?" Until I said this, I wasn't even sure I was going to do what Andy asked. But now I've said it. I guess I am. My chest tightens with excitement.

"Oh, Lizzy." Ryan groans and scrabbles his hand through his hair. "Always something, it is."

"I know. Sorry. Please? Andy Masters."

"Their family just moved here? Jason Masters' younger brother? The house that looks like a castle by the water, with the zip line and the trampoline in the backyard?"

"Right."

"I think their dad is a vice-president at High's Hardware. Beaucoup bucks. I didn't know you hung out with him."

"Yep." My stomach wobbles a little. Does Ryan think he's out of my league, too?

Ryan turns into the neighborhood, driving between two large stone gates surrounded by sprawling flowerbeds, perfectly maintained. We weave through the neighborhood of towering stone mansions, one bigger than the next.

"Jason Masters is incredibly competitive. He holds the state record for breast stroke."

"Yeah, Andy sometimes jokes about that."

"Oh, like his brother is great with women?"

"I guess. And there's the younger brother who's won like, three science fairs back in New Jersey where they used to live."

"Everyone in Andy's family picks something and excels at it, it seems," Ryan says. "Maybe there's a lot of pressure at home.

Maybe it isn't always a walk in the park, living in a house like a castle."

"This is it," I say, as Ryan comes up on a quiet, elegant cul-de-sac.

"Now see, I think that turret is just too, too much," he says, pulling the car around.

I look for a car in the driveway or bicycle parked in the yard and don't see one. "Be right back." I jump out. My whole body reverberates with the expectation of seeing Andy, seeing his house, doing this ultra-secret favor for him.

"What about the book?" Ryan says, knitting his brows at me.

"Oh! Yeah." I pull my Health book from my worn backpack. Why did I lie? Now I have to leave it at Andy's house and then I won't have it in class tomorrow. Plus I'm still going to have to ask Ryan to take the memory card to Billy Z's house. I am such a dork. I have transformed into a liar and a sneak in one single week. I don't even recognize myself.

I study the flowers planted in the shade under a tree in Andy's front yard. Mom has told me these delicate little blue flowers are called "forget-me-nots," and they seem to be the perfect flower to be planted outside Andy's house since I seem to forget everything—including even being a decent person—because of him.

A shiver races along my hairline as I climb his porch steps and ring the bell, staring at myself in the cut glass pattern on the front door. Inside, I hear footsteps and talking. My throat tightens. I squelch a sudden desire to run back to the car.

The deadbolt slides back with a heavy click. I hold my breath. Andy opens the door, talking on his phone, and he waves me in, pacing. He wears baggy jeans and a faded navy T-shirt that says "College" with a hole under one arm. He's skinny, anyway, and the old, shapeless clothes make him look even skinnier.

Feeling kind of stupid, I step onto the white marble of the front hall and then onto a thick oriental rug that I'm sure cost thousands of dollars. I am still barefoot and my toenails are painted with scraps of pink polish from several weeks ago. A spiral staircase curves up to the white-carpeted second floor. The front hall smells like furniture polish. A golden retriever with a graying muzzle wanders in and sniffs my leg, waves its tail, and leaves.

"Yeah," Andy says into the phone, holding up one finger as to ask me to wait. "I got the interview today at my house after they suspended me. Lizzy's bringing it over. Just keep with our plan, OK?

Plan?

"OK, Lizzy is here and she'll bring you the memory card. I'm giving it to her right now. Talk to you later."

Andy shoves his cell into his back pocket. His dark curls stick up a bit more than usual and his eyes have kind of a crazy flash to them. He grabs a memory card from the front hall table and holds it in his palm. "Hey, Lizzy, thanks for doing this. You never texted me back so I wasn't sure you were going to do it."

"I got my phone taken away at school today. While I was trying to text you."

"Oh, that's a major bummer. Well, all you have to do is take this over to Billy Z's, right on your way home. Remember, this is like plutonium." He cradles the memory card gently. "Like you're carrying plutonium."

I take the card and stare at it like the secret of life is written on it. "Andy," I say. "What's on this thing?"

He makes a zipping motion over his lips. "It's totally top secret until I break the story tomorrow on *The WLHS Show.*"

I take a step back. "What are you doing, Andy?"

"I don't know what you mean, Lizzy. I'm doing what reporters do. I'm getting the story."

"Yeah, but where is the story coming from? " I actually don't know what I'm saying. In so many ways, I don't want to know what comes next.

His mouth drops open. "Lizzy, I thought you were with me here. What'd you come here for if you're going to be like that about it?"

"Andy, I came here because we're friends and I care about you and it just seems as though you might be getting into something really serious. If you know who it is, or if you're somehow involved—this is not just a prank anymore. You could get expelled."

His hands drop to his sides and he looks disgusted and heartbroken. "This is not what you think."

I stare at the memory card, and take a deep breath. "I mean, you didn't stage the prank fire drills, did you? Or to make some kind of point about whether our school is ready for things like this or how the honor code will never really work?"

The Camry's horn blows in the driveway. I push open the storm door and poke my head out.

"Lizzy!" Ryan leans out the window. "C'mon, what's taking so long?"

I turn back to Andy, who stares into my eyes. His eyelids look reddish around the edges. "Let me get this straight. You think *I* might be doing the April Fools' pranks?"

And as always with Andy I feel like I've been pulled into a magnetic field of some kind, some vortex that makes me do and say things I'd never do and say otherwise. I stand there with the Health book, shifting my weight from one leg to another. "You're just so...into it."

He stares at me. "How can you be thinking about hanging out with me at the dance tomorrow night if you think that?"

My heart beats so hard right now it feels like it might break one of my ribs. "It's just...if you even know who did it, you're supposed to tell. Not do top secret interviews with the person."

"Give me back the memory card." He holds out his hand.

Fast as lightning, I pull it closer to me. "No, I'll do it. Just don't tell me who you interviewed or what they said." My heart flutters, and there's a buzzing in my head and I almost forget to give him the Health book, but at the last minute I shove it at him, then nearly trip down the step from his front porch. I run toward the car and slide into the front seat. I can ride my bike to Billy Z's later. It's too risky to ask Ryan to stop.

"What took you so long?" he asks. "And what happened? You're all red."

"Nothing." I pinch my upper lip between my teeth. Tears leak out of the corners of my eyes for the second time today.

He studies me. "Fool me, you can't. Andy Masters is Mr. Pomme Frite, isn't he?"

I nod my head.

Ryan reaches to check my seat beat. As we drive away, it occurs to me that Andy paid no attention when I said I cared about him. No attention at all. Tomorrow night's dance seems a million miles away in another place in time.

Whatever was about to happen between Andy and me is obviously over.

CHAPTER ELEVEN

I AM ON MY BIKE, with the memory card in a plastic baggie in my pocket, headed up the street to Billy Z's, and listening on my phone to every really desperate emo song I can think of. Now, thinking back over all the reasons why I thought Andy might be involved, those reasons seem stupid. He was late to class both times we had the pranks. That could have been a total coincidence. He was excited about interviewing the cops. Big deal; anyone in his position would be. He got me to create a diversion while he went back in the school, supposedly to interview the cops. He made a few comments about how the pranks made the week at school so much more interesting. Does all of that add up to anything? I just don't know what to think.

A block down the street, Mom's silver Honda stops beside me and I try not to frown. She rolls down the window. "Lizzy! I got the job!"

"Hey, congratulations!" I smile. This should be great news for our family but all I can think about is Andy and getting to Billy Z's.

She looks expectant and confident—expressions I haven't

seen on her face for a long time —and relief floods through me. She's wearing the new slacks, jacket and top she modeled for us a few days ago. Maybe she wasn't mad at me. Maybe she was just mad because she couldn't get a job.

She reaches over to the passenger seat and holds up a white plastic helmet. "Check out my helmet for driving the forklift. My boss told me I could bring it home to show you and Ryan."

"Cool." I stretch my smile as my heart thuds.

"Where are you going?"

"Oh, just out for a bike ride. I won't be gone long." My foot is poised on the pedal.

"No, not now, sweetie. I want us to go out to dinner to celebrate. I just texted Dad, and he's on his way home. Come on, let's get ready and go."

I chew my lip. We haven't gone out to dinner in a long time. One of my favorite things to do when we're out to dinner is check out the dining room to see if anyone might need the Heimlich maneuver.

"I'll be ready in time." I squeeze the brakes nervously. The memory card seems to throb in my back pocket. "Just a short ride?"

"No, Lizzy, we need to go early because I got an email from the principal and there's a parent meeting about the April Fools' pranks at the school tonight at seven-thirty."

"I can still make it. I'm just going on a fifteen-minute ride."

"No, there's not time for that."

"Mom, come on, it's not a big deal."

"I said no, Lizzy!"

Panic and anger shoot through me. "I have to!"

"Why in the world would you have to go on a bike ride? Where's your flour baby, anyway? You didn't lose it, did you?"

Adrenalin shoots under my skin as I realize I don't have fourth-dynasty Ziggy. I left her sitting on my bed, leaning slightly, with her trusting lopsided grin. She really cannot go anywhere without me. "She's upstairs on my bed," I say.

"Aren't you supposed to take that flour baby EVERYWHERE you go for a full week? What if it was really your baby? Come inside now and get ready." Mom smiles, raises her eyebrows, and accelerates toward our driveway.

Furious and defeated, I turn my bike around and pedal back to the house. Somehow, I will have to take the card to Billy Z later. Maybe while Mom and Dad are at the school meeting.

———

Forty-five minutes later Dad, Mom, Ryan and I slide into a high-backed booth at our favorite neighborhood Mexican restaurant. Large, bright vistas of desert-like Mexican landscape stretch around the walls populated with men wearing sombreros and women in long skirts gaily painted with red, yellow, and teal flowers. The restaurant's sound system pipes out cheerful Mexican tunes with peppy violins and guitars. Dad's nickname for this restaurant is "El Telepathic Taco," because the food comes so fast it's almost as though we don't have to order it; we just think about what we want to eat on the way and bam! it's there, hot and steaming, when we arrive.

I put Ziggy on the table, snug against the wall of the booth. Before we are adequately settled, a fast-moving waiter with shiny dark hair places a basket of tortilla chips and a bowl of salsa on the table.

"*Gracias*," Ryan says.

"*De nada*," says the waiter, and as he jogs away we all reach for the chips at once.

I try to make myself stop thinking about Andy and the memory card. Out of habit, I scan the booths and tables to see if anyone might be choking and need medical assistance. At

Camp Med, I was among the best at the Heimlich maneuver. Mentally, I calculate when we will get home from dinner, how long Mom and Dad will be gone to the school meeting, and what I should tell Ryan when I head out on my bike.

"Honey, tell us about your interview," Dad says to Mom, putting his arm around her. "This is major."

"Well." Mom dips a chip into the salsa. "I met with the warehouse owner, a Mr. Sebastiano. He started explaining that driving the forklift was tricky. Then I said I had no doubt I could learn to drive one. And he said, well, there is also heavy lifting, and I said that I'd been lifting kids and boxes of library books for years. I said, 'You want to hire a man, don't you?' And I gave him my look. You know my look?"

"Yeah." All three of us answer at once.

"And he said, 'No, no, it's not that I want to hire a man, that's not it.'"

"But that *was* it, wasn't it?" says Dad.

"Right, and I said, 'Mr. Sebastiano, hire me. I will prove to you that I can do this job.' And he said, 'Could you excuse me for a minute?' I went outside and stood in the hallway—I almost turned into a puddle of nervous sweat—and I heard him talking on the phone and then he called me back in and said, 'When can you start?'"

"Yes!" Dad pumps his arm in the air and then gives Mom a kiss on the cheek. "Time to celebrate!"

A server in a peasant blouse and flowered skirt appears beside our booth. "Are you ready to order?" she says.

"I'll have number three," Mom says cheerfully, then glances up from the menu. "What about you kids? Lizzy, is something wrong?"

"No, no." I quickly order my favorite—fish tacos.

"*Yo quiero Numero Diez y siete, por favor,*" Ryan says, with a rueful smile. "*Muchas gracias.*"

"*De nada.*" The server smiles at Ryan, scribbles on the order pad, and looks at Dad.

"Number Seven," Dad says. As our server leaves, he looks at his watch. "Okay, our order should be here. What's taking so long?"

Mom laughs and shoves her shoulder into Dad's. She is in such a good mood now, and I find their lame repetitive jokes reassuring.

"So," says Ryan. "When do you learn to drive the forklift?"

"Mr. Sebastiano said he'd teach me tomorrow. It's an old one and sometimes is hard to get running. He said so far every employee he's hired has poked a hole in the wall. So my goal is to be the first one not to do that."

Dad lifts his water glass. "Here's to Mom not poking a hole in the wall."

"Hear, hear," Ryan says. We clink our water glasses together.

"Things are going to be different around our house now," Mom says. "We'll go out to dinner more. We'll go on a vacation. Where should we go?"

"Paris!" I say, because Marisa's family went there last spring break and she told me it was the most beautiful city she had ever seen.

"Wales!" says Ryan. "The home of the once and future king."

Dad's eyes flicker. "Let's start a bit smaller. How does the beach sound?"

"The beach sounds great," I say, swinging my feet.

"Good! Lizzy, I have to say, I am pleasantly surprised by your level of responsibility with your flour baby," Mom says.

Ryan selects a large chip and dips it carefully into the salsa, giving me a sidelong glance and humming the theme to "Jaws" under his breath.

"Thanks." I smile at Mom, then kick Ryan's ankle.

"You did a nice job on her eyes," she tells me.

"Exceptional job on the eyes," says Ryan.

I kick him again. "Thanks." I can't look at Mom.

She focuses on me more closely. "It's really disconcerting that they haven't been able to catch that kid doing the pranks."

"They're interviewing everyone in the computer club and who has classes in or near the computer lab," I say. Suddenly I wonder if they will interview me.

"Lizzy, who's driving you girls to the competition this weekend?" Dad asks. "Do you need me to drive you?"

Heat crawls up my neck. I can't tell them about missing the competition. Not yet. "No, you don't need to drive, Dad. I think Marisa's mom is."

Just then, to my great relief, Dad gets a phone call. As he gets up to leave the table, he says something into the phone about a blood drive.

Mom stands up. "I need to wash my hands before our food gets here. I'll be right back."

As soon as they've both left, Ryan glares at me. "Lizzy, what is going on with you?"

I glare back. "Nothing."

"Too well, I know you. What is it?"

I glance across the busy restaurant. The door to the ladies' room has a woman in a long flowered skirt painted on it. "I don't have time to tell you now; Mom will be back."

"It's about Mr. Pomme Frite, isn't it? Talk fast."

I take a deep breath. "He wanted me to do something for him and, well, I said yes."

"What? What did you say you would do?"

I stare at the door to the ladies room, and at Dad standing outside the glass door to the restaurant, on the phone, then look at my lap. "I...."

The door to the ladies room opens and Mom reappears.

I let out the breath. "Too late."

Just as Mom slides back into the booth, our server appears with steaming platters stacked to her elbow of cheese-topped tacos, sour cream, guacamole, and refried beans.

"Enjoy your meal," our server says.

Dad rejoins us, and for a few minutes the only sound is our forks scraping our plates and the ice cubes tinkling in our water glasses.

Just then, out of the corner of my eye, I see a woman at the next table lean her head back with a gasp. It looks like she's choking. Oh my gosh, this is it—time for the Heimlich maneuver! This is my chance! I slide from our booth in one smooth motion and in seconds I'm standing behind her.

With efficiency and power that I'm incredibly proud of, I wrap my arms tightly under her boobs and forcefully lift up.

"A-choo!" She sneezes loudly into a tissue a split second later.

Everyone at her table stares at me.

"Oh..." I let go of her boobs, which are somewhat large and damp, and step back. The heat of shame envelopes my entire body. "I'm sorry, I thought you were choking. I was...doing the Heimlich maneuver."

Laughter ricochets around the room and I dearly wish for a trapdoor to open in the floor and swallow me. There is a smattering of applause mixed with the laughter. After a few seconds of mortifying confusion, the lady turns and I see her bright red hair and her too-pale face and do a double-take—it's Mrs. Vangraff, the mom I'm babysitting for Saturday night!

"Mrs. Vangraff!" Oh my gosh, I grabbed Mrs. Vangraff's boobs! My face must be glowing, it feels so hot. "Again, I'm so sorry!"

"Lizzy! It's fine, no harm done, I know you were trying to help." She pats my arm a little awkwardly.

Next to her, a red-cheeked baby, who must be Casey, starts to cry. I feel so stupid, I'd like to cry, too. Little whimpers escalate to sobbing, then wailing so loud my ears pound and my brainwaves scramble. This is enough to induce temporary blindness. Mrs. Vangraff tries to put the pacifier in his mouth, says, "Shhh, shhh," but Casey just won't stop. His wailing goes on and on until practically everyone in the restaurant has put down their forks.

My heart sinks. Clearly, I should never have agreed to babysit for him. Not to mention grab his mom's boobs.

At last Mrs. Vangraff slides out of her chair and swoops Casey up. "I'll take him outside," she says.

Mrs. Vangraff's hair is awry and she has spit-up on her shirt. Casey's face is as red as a tomato, smeared with tears. Mrs. Vangraff holds the howling Casey close to her body, rocking him. She glances over at my family. "Hi, Ellen, hi Wayne, hi Ryan. He was quiet earlier and we were desperate to get out of the house."

Casey pounds his heels into his mother's hips, writhes and wriggles and squirms to escape her arms. He twists his body like a contortionist, arches his back and flings his arms and wails.

"I'm taking him right out!" She rushes away, tossing over her shoulder, "See you Saturday night, Lizzy. Casey can't wait!"

I slink back into my chair and the four of us sit for a moment in the blessed quiet, letting our ears decompress. My forearms are still damp from being under Mrs. Van Graff's boobs.

"Lizzy," Ryan says, laughing. "Casey can't *wait* for Saturday night."

"Lizzy, what in the..." Mom starts.

"Ellen, she was trying to help," Dad puts his hand on top of hers with a meaningful look, and Mom is quiet. "Good try, Lizzy," he says.

Besides still being embarrassed, I feel grateful to dad for sticking up for me. Yet if he knew everything I've done this week he might not be doing that.

———

When we get back from dinner I wait for Mom and Dad to leave for the meeting at the school to try again to ride my bike to Billy Z's house. But Dad says he has too much work to do for the Red Cross Board, and Mom goes alone. I start to panic. When am I going to take it?

I have no choice: I will have to go after Mom and Dad go to bed.

I text Billy Z and tell him that I have the memory card and will bring it later tonight, around midnight.

Ok, he texts back. I picture him, sitting at the computer, rearing back in the chair, as his dark, nimble fingers fly over the keyboard.

The garage door opens and Mom comes in from the meeting. Her voice and Dad's rumble downstairs as they discuss what was said. I crawl into bed with my clothes still on. The moon shines blue through the window and I can hear Ryan next door, in his bedroom, as his fingers tap faintly and erratically on his keyboard like faraway machine gun fire. He knocked on my door once tonight but I told him to go away. I can't talk to him. It's like his eyes coat me in truth serum. He'll make me tell him everything.

Mom doesn't come in my room to kiss me every night anymore and tonight I hope she doesn't. But a pie-shaped cone of light from the hallway slices across my bed and then stretches to include Ziggy's puffy little form sitting on my desk. Her silhouette fills the doorway.

Mom comes inside and sits on my bed beside me, looking at Ziggy, then squeezes my toes through the covers. "There were a lot of parents at that meeting tonight. Goodness, some people are really upset. They were shouting and pointing their fingers. It's been in all the local papers. The police and the administration got pretty defensive. They gave us this sheet with the website to go to if we have any information." She lays the sheet on my desk.

"Wow." I stay very still. Will Mom notice that I have on a T-shirt instead of my PJs?

"You understand how important it is to share any and all information you might have, don't you, Lizzy?"

"Yes, yes," I say tiredly, but in my head I see Andy's face.

"Okay, I know you understand. They assured us that all reports are completely anonymous." Mom gently runs her fingers over my forehead and temples. "And if you're scared, talk to us."

I nod, and she leaves, but I know I'm not going to talk to them. Not about losing the flour babies, not about going to Billy Z's tonight. In fact, I'm lying to my parents in ways that I never have before. I never even told them about detention. Because of Andy. At this rate, where would I start?

Maybe Kelly and I, when we made our pact about not making fools of ourselves over boys, were right all along. But now it's too late. I can't stop liking Andy, and I'm so crazy about him that I can't stop trying to help him.

An hour later, I get up. I check my phone for a text from Andy. Nothing. The moon's harsh light streams through my bedroom window, sharpening the edge of my computer's sleeping monitor. Is he ghosting me?

Seconds crawl by. Does he just trust me to go to Billy Z's?

All I need to do is slide the memory card into my computer and maybe I'll know who's been doing the pranks. I grip it so tight it almost cuts into my palm.

With a deep breath, I sit in the desk chair, and touch the keyboard. The screen saver disappears. I check again to see if Andy has texted. Nope.

Why was he so excited about the pranks?

Why was he late to class both days?

My heart hammers in my chest and I think about the heart in our fetal pig, what a hard, tough little fist it is.

I look at the sheet Mom left on my desk with the number to call with information. I look away.

I slide the memory card into the bay. A few more beats of my heart and all I will have to do is click to see.

I believe in what Mrs. Cruz and Miss Bebe said. It is my civic duty to tell if I think I know anything.

A long slow second drags by and I hold my breath. I remember standing in the stairwell and Andy whispering into my ear, the warmth of his breath on my hair.

I can't look. I don't want to know.

I pull the memory card free and leave the room, knowing I will never be an investigative journalist or private detective or any of those things. I choose to do what Andy asked me to do, and to keep not knowing.

I've never snuck out before. But, for Andy, I'll do it.

I purposefully left my bike outside the garage before dinner so I wouldn't have to open the garage door tonight and make a racket and wake everyone up. Of course, I'm not taking Ziggy with me. She is sitting safe on my desk. The truth: If she were a real baby, I would be staying home with her.

I tiptoe down the stairs, open the front door one centimeter at a time, then close it as softly as the landing of a feather. Then I tiptoe through the front yard, my breath ragged in the damp air. The moon is not quite full and beneath it dew gleams on the dark grass. Our trees resemble ancient bearded beings. From the silhouette of a nearby branch comes a repeated cry of an owl. A shiver runs along my skin, but I shake it off. I slide the memory card into my back pocket and push the bike down the driveway. The faint rhythmic "click, click" as the wheel spokes rotate twists the knot in my stomach tighter with every step.

Moments later I'm flying through the streets of our neighborhood. Wind whips my long hair behind me, grasps at my shirt, and coaxes cold tears from the corners of my eyes. A man suddenly approaches on the side of the road. I almost have a heart attack, and veer to the other side of the street. I see a small animal near the man and realize, with embarrassment, that he is just out walking his dog.

At the entrance of our neighborhood, I turn right onto the main road. I only have to stay on this for a few hundred yards, riding under the cone of the streetlights, and then I make a left into Billy Z's neighborhood. It's an average suburban Mooresville neighborhood, very similar to ours. Soon I glide to a stop in front of his house. Except for one dim light in an upstairs bedroom, it's dark. That must be his room. I text him, as we agreed, though it's not easy with shaking fingers.

Moments later the front door opens very slowly and he runs barefoot across the grass. "You got it?"

I can't see his face in the dark. "Yeah." I hold out the memory card.

"About time." He doesn't say "thanks," and he doesn't ask me if I looked. He just takes the card and jogs back through the yard. A second later the front door closes, and I'm sitting on the street at midnight alone on my bike.

I text Andy: **Done**.

Well, I did it. Slowly, shivering, I start to pedal home. It's not long before headlights are shining on me and I hear rolling tires following me slowly. I gasp and start riding my bike faster. The car keeps up, but doesn't pass me.

Is Dad out looking for me? I am starting to hyperventilate. I quickly turn down our cul-de-sac. The car follows me. Oh my God, what should I do?

I fly down the hill but the car pulls up beside me at the bottom.

"Young lady, it's mighty late to be out riding your bike."

I dare to glance over. Oh my God, it's a cop. In fact, it's Officer Egan, one of the cops that I've seen around the school this week, a square-faced white guy about my dad's age.

"Oh, I had to give somebody something for school," I say. I stop my bike and stand straddling it, my knees trembling so hard I am afraid I will fall down.

"Lending someone your notes or something like that?" Officer Egan asks.

"Yes." My voice sounds like a squeak.

"Well, why don't I escort you back to your house? Make sure you get home all right?"

"Oh, that's okay. I'm almost home."

"I insist." He gives me a hard look.

Slowly I pedal home with Officer Egan riding alongside. When I pedal down the driveway he follows me, and when I park my bike outside the garage he gets out of the car and shuts the door very quietly.

"Let's go in the front door," he says, stepping onto the front stoop.

"I have my key," I say. I hesitate and plead with him. "Please don't ring the doorbell. My parents are going to be so mad at me."

He gives me another hard look. "As well they should. You shouldn't be out riding around this time of night." Officer Egan reaches out to ring the doorbell and I feel so nauseated I am about to throw up.

Suddenly the door opens and Ryan is standing there.

"Hello, Lizzy. You're back, great," he says. "Hello, Officer Egan."

Officer Egan looks confused, and then he smiles. "Ryan! The yearbook editor."

"Yessir. That picture I took of you turned out pretty good."

Officer Egan looks pleased. "Oh, good." He hesitates. "So, you knew she was out?"

"Yes, one of her friends called in panic because she'd forgotten her math notes from school. There's some big test tomorrow, right Lizzy?" Ryan cocks his head at me.

"Right," I say.

"I told her I'd go with her, but she insisted she'd be quick."

Officer Egan looks at Ryan and then at me for a long moment, his eyes inscrutable in the darkness. Then, finally, he says, "Math, huh?"

"Lizzie can't stand to leave a friend in need, you know?"

I think Ryan's laying it on thick, but Officer Egan looks over at me and raises an eyebrow.

"It's good to help your friends," he says. "But no more joy rides in the middle of the night, agreed?"

"Yessir." I step inside with Ryan. "Thank you, sir," I say with a hopeful smile.

"I'm going to hold you to it. See you at school tomorrow." He gives us a salute and returns to his car. Again, he shuts the door with only a faint "click," and glides away without even turning on his headlights.

As I tiptoe up the stairs behind Ryan, relief floods through me like ice water.

"Thank you," I whisper.

That was close. Too close.

———

Ryan follows me into my room.

"Gimme a break, Lizzy," he says. "Talk."

I don't say anything.

Ryan blinks once and stares at me. He looks like that owl I heard. "Where did you just go?" he hisses.

"To help Mr. Pomme Frite," I finally say. "I started suspecting him of staging the pranks at school. But then he asked me to do something for him and...I did."

Ryan plops onto the end of my bed. The moon paints the dirty blond squiggles of his hair. I imagine it does the same thing to mine. "What did you do?"

"He got some kind of interview that has something to do with the pranks, and he got suspended, and then grounded, and so he needed me to take the memory card to Billy Z, one of the other kids who works on *The WLHS Show*."

"Lizzy!" Ryan huffs air through his teeth. "And why do you suspect him of staging the pranks?"

"All I know is that he was late to class both days when we had the prank fire drills. And he's very excited about investigating the whole thing for *The WLHS Show*. And he asked me to create a diversion during one of the evacuations so that he could go back into the school to do an interview." I chew my thumbnail. "I feel terrible. I can't believe I have such a crush on him and suspect him at the same time. "

"Is there any way you can get proof that he did it?"

"I have absolutely no real proof. I think my imagination just went crazy, that's all."

"But what about the honor code? Aren't you supposed to

turn in any suspects? And what about what you've done? You could be an accessory!"

I turn on my side, away from him. "Andy asked me for my help. And I gave it. I just still...have these suspicions."

"But what if you were right? What if he *did* do it? Then you have a responsibility to tell what you know."

I pull my pillow over my head. "He's already been suspended. Do you have any idea how much you sound like Mom? Ryan, I have no proof. And I don't want to do anything to hurt Andy. "

He is silent. My heart beats painfully. If only Andy would send me one measly text.

Ryan frowns. "Lizzy, you have to turn him in. I don't care if his father is the vice-president of High's Hardware, I don't care if he lives in a castle, and I don't care if you have a huge crush on him. It's the right thing to do."

I close my eyes. A heavy silence settles between us, and then I hear the doorknob turn as he starts to leave the room.

"Ryan?"

"What?"

"You won't tell Mom?"

"I won't tell Mom."

I don't think I'm going to be able to go to sleep. I get up, wander into the bathroom and stare at myself in the mirror. I always look forlorn in the middle of the night, with my hair all messy and my near-sighted droopy eyes.

I check the sides of my nose for blackheads, then examine the hairs inside my nostrils. I try various smiles. They all look fake. I examine the red tissue on the inside of my lower eyelid. Yuck. Everything seems strange late at night. It's as though I don't recognize this conglomeration of strange parts as my own.

I go back in my room and lie there for a few minutes, picking at the skin on my lip.

Why hasn't Andy texted me back, at least to let me know he got my text? I know he was mad at me, but I guess I hoped that if I delivered the memory card, he'd forgive me and see that I was on his side. I text him again, then watch the screen of my phone for a long minute, then its light goes off.

Minutes creep by. Nothing.

My thoughts begin to race. He obviously didn't think that I needed anything from him to go through with this. He obviously isn't grateful for what I've done for him, for the trouble I've gone to. For the risks I've taken. He's just ghosting me, like I don't matter, like I don't exist, like, as Kelly said, I'm out of my league. Maybe all of this *has* been a prank.

How can he do this to me? Furious tears well in my eyes.

He was the very first boy who ever even asked for my number. And now, after I've sneaked out and taken a huge risk for him, after less than a week, he's ghosting me.

Anger floods me all the way to my fingertips and I pick up the sheet Mom left on my desk and find the anonymous reporting website on my laptop. I can either call or email, but I don't want to call because Ryan might hear me talking. It asks me if I'd like to remain anonymous. As I type "yes," my trembling fingers sweat onto the keys. Will it really be anonymous? The site says yes, because of encryption technology. Then it asks for my report.

I take a deep breath. Ryan told me to do this. He drives me crazy sometimes, but he's a good big brother and he looks out for me.

"I don't know whether I'm right or not," I type. "And I don't actually have any proof. But Andy Masters was late to class twice when we had the fire drill pranks this week, and he asked me to create a diversion so he could go back inside the school and interview people. He also asked me to take a memory chip to another student when he was suspended. I don't know what was on the memory chip, but I did take it."

It occurs to me that I might be getting myself into trouble by writing this. But it's too late now.

The website gives me a password and thanks me for the information.

I can't believe what I've done. I've reported Andy. I have this feeling that I'm sinking straight to hell.

CHAPTER TWELVE

FRIDAY

"MOM, I THINK I'M SICK." I shuffle into the kitchen in the early morning gloom, still in my PJs. I don't want to go to school. My stomach and head both hurt. It could be both appendicitis and a brain tumor at the same time. Or idiopathic thrombocytopenic purpura. I could barely get myself out of bed. I can't face Andy. I can't face anyone.

Mom cocks her head, dressed in her forklift-driving jumpsuit, and gives me a skeptical look. "Lizzy, you can't do that to me. This is my first day of work. Get dressed. You have to go to school."

Thirty minutes later, I'm on the bus. When it careens around a corner, it jostles Kelly into my shoulder and tosses Marie Curie into my lap. Marie Curie looks bedraggled. The batteries in the little flashlight that represents radium have died. Kelly put tape over a small hole in Marie's cheek to keep flour from seeping out. Some joker took a bite out of the cinnamon roll Kelly was using for Marie's bun.

When I hand Marie back, and point this out, Kelly says, "I know, it was Brian Williams. I hope he comes down with botulism."

"Can you get botulism from bread?"

Harrison's sharp-boned face comes between us. "Botulism comes from home-canned foods."

I quickly look it up on *Five Minute Med Consult*. Of course, Harrison is right.

"The pancreas is the one that looked like feta cheese, right?" Kelly asks. She's opened her notebook to the diagram of the fetal pig.

OMG! Today is our fetal pig test! I forgot to study!

My shock is so great that I think I'm going to faint.

"I forgot to study for the test!" I tell Kelly. "Oh, no!"

Her mouth drops open. "You're kidding me!"

I think I can actually feel the blood draining out of my head and into my feet. This has never happened before. I have never FORGOTTEN to study. What is the matter with me?

In a panic I grab the notes Harrison sent us the other night and start madly reading through them. They are incredibly detailed and helpful. I picture him, grown-up, with his thin white fingers, as a misunderstood chemist. As I read and remember each organ, I am so glad I forced myself to do the dissection and didn't chicken out. Visualizing my own hands with the probe helps me remember. I close my eyes and walk through, imagining each one. Esophagus, larynx, trachea, bronchus, lungs. Duodenum, gallbladder, large intestine, pancreas, small intestine, stomach. Liver, posterior vena cava, thymus, thyroid. Heart. Excretory system. Circulatory system. And reproductive system.

I am jerked back into the present as the bus screeches to a stop and two guys from the baseball team stomp down the aisle, their cleats hanging over their shoulders by dirty, knotted strings. They make me think of Andy and my heart hurts. Tonight is the dance. It's pretty obvious by now that he will never speak to me again, much less want me to come to the dance with him.

One of the baseball players steps on Harrison's foot on purpose before swinging into the seats near Gordon.

"Hey!" Harrison turns around and tries to shove the baseball player and the Mrs. McCready shouts, "No fighting, Harrison!"

Harrison flings himself into his seat and stares out the window.

I have to admit, I feel sorry for him. He was only trying to fight back.

I catch the baseball player's eye. "Ass," I say. He shoots me the bird. I shoot one right back. It feels pretty darn good.

Kelly runs her hand over her bun and heaves a sigh. "Statistics say that the pranker is eighty percent more likely to be a male."

"I'm sick of everybody talking about it," I make sure my voice sounds as bored as possible. "Anyway, I have to study." How am I going to memorize all this between now and class?

"On the contrary, I find it fascinating," Kelly says. "I can't stop thinking about it. I'm assembling a grid, in fact, similar to the one you use when you play *Clue,* to help rule out certain suspects."

"You're kidding." I can't believe Kelly is doing this.

"Would you like to see it?"

"Not really." She gives me a hurt look, so I add, "Sure."

With a furtive glance back at Harrison, Kelly opens one of her enormous notebooks and withdraws a sheet of pale green graph paper with names neatly printed down one side. Along the top margin is a list of attributes, such as "alibi," "class in or near computer room," and "history of behavior issues."

"Gosh, this seems like a lot." I glance down the list. Andy's name is on it. So is Lance Spock's. Harrison's is there, too, but Kelly quickly covers it up with the edge of her book when he peers over the seat. She points at Lance's name. "My prime suspect."

"No!" I say. "It's not him. He's a decent guy. Just because he does those drawings on his arms, people think he's sketchy. He's really kind of sweet, kind of in a daze."

"How do you know him?"

"I was in detention with him the other day."

Kelly nods sagely. "Aha. Excellent location for acquiring character references."

I put my thumb and forefinger over my eyes just like I've seen my dad do when he's frustrated by how narrow-minded people can be. "I promise you, it's not him."

"What about Andy?" Kelly probes.

Anger washes over me, as I think again about the way Andy has been ghosting me. "Who knows? Maybe it is."

And then, oh my gosh, I wish I hadn't said a thing.

Kelly narrows her eyes. "What do you mean? Are you guys still talking?"

I shrug. "Do you still think he's out of my league? And that he asked me to the dance as an April Fools' prank?"

Kelly hesitates. "N-no." She looks at her lap, and plays with Marie Curie's flashlight. "I shouldn't have said that, Lizzy. I'm sorry. But one thing maybe you haven't realized is that you have a new best friend AND a boyfriend and I don't."

I catch my breath. I can't believe Kelly has apologized. And I also can't believe that until this moment I hadn't been able to see things from her point of view. "Oh." I am speechless. I think about all the times that she's probably watched me walk down the hall with Marisa or sit with Marisa in the cafeteria, remembering when we used to be together. "I'm sorry, too," I say. "But just because I'm friends with Marisa doesn't mean you and I aren't still friends."

"You and I both know that a person can only have one best friend." Kelly is brutally honest, as usual. "But I talked to my mom about it and she said that it's natural for friendships to change as we get older."

I feel a little jealous, that she's able to talk to her mom about things. And I wonder about myself, about the way I wanted to belong so much to the cheerleaders, and then pretty much left other relationships behind. I have to face up to it—that is what I did. Maybe it's not a crime, but I'm not proud of myself.

"Well, I guess maybe our friendship has changed, but I hope we're still friends." The honest talk seems to have cleared the air some between Kelly and me, so I press on. "And Andy's not my boyfriend. We've only been texting for a week. Anyway, I'm positive the person that did it wasn't Andy." I hate lying to Kelly —we've just created a delicate new relationship. But if there is any question about who reported Andy, I don't want anyone to know it was me. I already majorly wish I hadn't.

At that moment, Harrison reaches over the seat and yanks Kelly's book away from the page, revealing his name.

"My name's on there! You suspect me!" Furious, he spikes the book onto the floor, throws his backpack across the aisle into the empty seat on the other side, and then, punching the back of our seat with his hand, slams into the other seat. Seething anger comes from his eyes.

Kelly and I both duck, afraid he might throw something at us.

"Harrison hit our seat!" Kelly calls to the bus driver.

The baseball players laugh and use high-pitched singsong voices to mimic her, saying, "Harrison hit our seat! Harrison hit our seat!" Because they are baseball players and Andy plays baseball, I hate them.

Mrs. McCready looks at us in the rearview mirror, exhaustion darkening her heavy face. "Stop hitting their seat," she yells to Harrison. "Right now."

———

Twenty minutes later, I head into homeroom, cradling Ziggy IV in my arms. I pass one of the police officers in the hall, and my hearts starts an irregular beat. I half expect him to accost me and say, "So you're the one who reported Andy Masters!" but he just passes without even noticing me. Maybe that reporting system really *is* anonymous.

A few minutes later I get paranoid again when Brian Williams, the football player from detention, passes me. He has never before acknowledged my existence, but today he holds up a hand and says, "Yo. Lizzy Borden."

At first I kind of like the fact that a popular football player has come up with a nickname for me since detention. But then I feel mad about what he's called me, like he thinks I'm trouble, just like Ms. Stokel said.

Today is the last day of the week of the flour babies. My last day with Ziggy IV. After today, I don't have to keep checking to make sure I've got her. I don't have to shield her from those harrowing drops of water at the water fountain that could melt her like the Wicked Witch of the West. I don't have to race out to the soccer field, after forgetting her, to search for her on the damp grass. And I don't have to sit at lunch or dinner with her on the table beside my plate, guarding against onslaughts of flying food.

No, today I can rip her open and mix her with eggs and milk or chocolate and make biscuits or cookies out of her. Or, if I want, I can take her out to the garage and toss her in the trash. The choice is mine.

I place her on my desk and stare into her Cleopatra eyes. She doesn't judge, or call me irresponsible, or hopeless. She doesn't tell me I'm out of my league. She wouldn't scream or yell if I left her somewhere. She would only wait patiently until I returned. She will not talk back or throw up on me or cry nonstop or kick me in the ribs, like Casey probably will on Saturday night. In short, she's much easier to get along with than a real person.

But I have to live with real people.

I grab for the notes Harrison sent us the other night and try to get a few minutes of review in during homeroom.

The screen in the corner of the classroom clicks on and the picture blooms. It's time for *The WLHS Show*. Time for Andy's mysterious interview. The scene opens with Andy at his house. I recognize his fancy foyer, remember standing there with my chipped toenail polish and grabbing the memory card from him. I remember trying not to burst into tears in front of Ryan. I hold my breath and watch.

"Welcome to *The WLHS Show*," he says. He's wearing that same T-shirt with the hole in it that says "College." "Today we have an exclusive interview. No one, except me and my audio technician, Billy Z, knows the identity of these people. Since I'm suspended from school today, these people offered to come to my house and speak with me about the situation with the April Fools' pranks in our school."

The scene changes to Andy's kitchen, a sunny octagonal room on the back of the house. Andy and Police Chief Flora Ballou sit at the oval oak table, bathed in strips of afternoon sun slanting through vertical blinds that cover the sliding glass door to the enormous back deck. Chief Ballou is a middle-aged black woman. She has shiny black hair cut in a bob and excellent posture. Our IT administrator, Mr. Joya, also sits at the table with Andy and Chief Ballou, his alert brown eyes moving from

Andy to Chief Ballou. He's not as young as Mr. Waggoner, but he's one of the youngest teachers in our school. His family's from Ecuador. Everyone is pretty much in awe of how smart he is.

Andy leans forward, his elbows on the table. "Thank you for coming to my house for this interview, Chief Ballou and Mr. Joya."

Chief Ballou and Mr. Joya? This was the exclusive interview? Not the pranker?

Heat rushes to my face. I feel horribly hoodwinked. And terrible that I turned Andy in! Creeping goosebumps start at my skull and travel down my neck and shoulders. A stubborn part of me stays mad at him, because he hasn't answered my text, even after I went to Billy Z's for him last night. But part of me feels flooded with guilt for betraying him. Why did I do it? Can I somehow undo it?

"Chief Ballou," Andy says. "What is your department doing to investigate the pranks?"

"First, Andy, let me say that I welcome the opportunity to speak directly to the students of Lakeside High about this very sensitive situation." Chief Ballou crosses her arms over her uniform. Her voice is no-nonsense. She clears her throat, and rolls her head from one shoulder to another like a boxer getting ready for a fight. "As you know, Andy, we have been interviewing students about their whereabouts during the time the pranks have occurred. We do know that these pranks originate from a remote computer outside the school and we feel confident that we will soon have an IP address. Whoever is doing the pranks clearly knows his or her way around a computer, so we will be interviewing everyone in the computer and gaming clubs. We have talked to a few students more than once. The IT administrator is looking at records and feels confident that he will be able to trace the IP address back to the perpetrator pretty soon."

"Once you catch the person, or people, what will happen to them?"

"We will arrest him or her. This is a very serious matter."

"Well, Chief Ballou, some people disagree. Some people say these are just pranks, no different from the kind of things that were done in the classic movie *Ferris Bueller's Day Off*. Some people say kids shouldn't be arrested for these kinds of things. What are your thoughts about that, Mr. Joya?

Mr. Joya leans toward Andy, his arms crossed on the table. "In the hacker world, these kids aren't black hats, I agree. These pranks are not malicious. They're just that—pranks."

"On the other hand," Chief Ballou interjects, "the police and fire departments have lost time in having to repeatedly come to your school. Real emergencies took place while our men and women assessed these pranks, and we were short manpower to help those in need. That is why false alarms are more than pranks—they're dangerous."

Andy turns. "Mr. Joya, how close are you to finding out who this is?"

"We've had all the teachers change their passwords, and taken some other precautions, so we are hopeful the fire alarms and cartoons will not happen again. We believe it's only a matter of time before we can identify the IP address. And once that happens, I will be having what I hope will be some very illuminating conversations with these students. I'm sure, to do this, these kids are very bright. If we could only tap into that. You know, maybe we could consider offering a class in the good and the bad that hacking can do for a community." Mr. Joya raises his eyebrows as he makes this suggestion.

Sighing, I sink into dull disappointment, realizing all of last night's anxiety was for nothing. Someone taps my arm. It's my homeroom teacher, Mr. Campbell, with his wide face, tan and weathered from too much time fishing on Lake Norman. "Ms. Robinson would like to see you in her classroom," he says, raising his eyebrows.

"Now?" I say. When he nods, I shoulder my backpack slowly, trying to keep watching Andy until the last possible minute. Then I pick up Ziggy and head for Ms. Robinson's classroom. Maybe this is about the day in detention. Or could it be about reporting Andy? But it couldn't. I was assured it was anonymous.

Still.

The freshman hall is mostly empty now. One guy stands beside an open locker with a stack of rumpled papers wedged in the bottom like a nest. My shoes squeak on the linoleum as I head down the quiet halls. I peer into the classrooms and see all the flour babies sitting on desks, shoved into backpacks, lying on the floor. They're dirty and wrinkled, leaking, tattered, and worn. Many are held together now with duct or packing tape. Flour babies that used to wear cute little outfits are now naked and dirty and partially smushed. It's true, taking good care of a flour baby for a whole week is no easy task.

Ziggy is among the cutest, if I do say so myself. Of course, she is a bit younger than the rest of them. Only two days old instead of five.

Ms. Robinson does not have students assigned to her during homeroom, and she is alone in her classroom. Her tall, stork-like frame bends over her desk, and as I step through the door she slashes red marks across someone's paper.

"You wanted to see me, Ms. Robinson?"

She looks up and I notice a row of squat shapes lined on her worktable. I just about wet my pants.

She caps her red pen with a decisive click, and crosses her arms. "Yes, Lizzy," she says, following my gaze.

Side by side on her worktable, in various stages of disrepair, stand Ziggy I, II and III. Ziggy I looks as though it might have been soaked with water and then stepped on. Ziggy II is smeared with dirt and grass stains. And Ziggy III looks like it has been run over.

Ms. Robinson stands now, and walks over to the work table. "Did you have any information you wanted to offer about this particular situation?"

The arm I'm using to hold Ziggy IV shakes, and I pull her closer.

I look at those three beaten-up flour babies. I feel like I'm going to throw up. How did they get here?

I give up. I am not a responsible person. I haven't been able to prove a thing to anyone.

Ms. Robinson taps her long narrow foot but doesn't speak.

I push my hair off my forehead. "I'm sorry." When I speak it sounds like a croak.

"You lost your flour baby."

"Yes, ma'am."

"You went and got another one as a substitute."

"Yes, ma'am."

"You lost the second one."

"Yes, ma'am."

"You replaced that one."

"Yes, ma'am." The rhythm wears on me, like a hammer pounding nails.

"The one in your arms now...that's your fourth. Or did you lose a few more?"

"No, this is the last Ziggy."

"Ziggy?"

"What I named her. Sort of like a zygote...a play on words." I sigh. "Never mind. Uh...where did you find them?"

"I found one on the soccer field after one of the school

evacuations. Another student turned in the other two this morning. "

I am about to cry, but I ask, "What student?"

"Harrison Atwell."

Harrison? Harrison found my flour babies, and then turned them in to Ms. Robinson instead of giving them back to me? Or...maybe he was taking my flour babies, and I didn't actually lose them. Anger wrenches my stomach tight and then races down my arms to the ends of my fingers, and I ball my hands into fists. "Ms. Robinson, I am not that irresponsible! I knew they were disappearing, but now I realize, I didn't lose them—he was taking them!"

Seconds tick by. Ms. Robinson stands to her full height, glaring down at me over her long sharp nose. "This is a serious accusation, Lizzy, do you understand? I'm not saying it's not possible."

"Yes, ma'am."

"But the fact remains that you have been lying to *me* all week about your flour baby."

Shame creeps down my body like a fast-growing vine. I know she's going to tell my parents. I think about the expressions of disappointment on their faces when they find out and I hardly feel like I can bear it.

"I ...I know, I'm sorry, Ms. Robinson. I just...didn't want to get in trouble for losing it. I mean, I have straight As. My parents are going to kill me."

"OK, well, having straight As is not more important than telling the truth, is it, Lizzy?"

"No, ma'am." I feel the burn of shame as I realize she is right.

"But there have been some extenuating circumstances in this case. Until we find out the truth about Harrison, I'll make a deal with you." She points her red pen at me, and takes long stork-like strides behind her desk. "I know that I told the class that anyone who loses his or her flour baby gets a zero, no exceptions. So you will get a zero on this assignment."

I feel like I'm about to drop through the floor. A zero. I have never before gotten a zero on an assignment. I feel myself flush as I think about Mom and Dad seeing this on the parent portal.

"A few other students lost them. The difference is, they came and told me. You tried to conceal it."

"Yes, ma'am."

"A limited number of mechanical babies are available. If you carry a mechanical baby for the weekend, I will give you extra credit."

I take a deep breath. It's not enough to bring my grade back to an A after the zero. But she is giving me another chance.

She raises her eyebrows, and I nod. It's my only chance.

She strides to the back of the classroom and takes a mechanical baby off the shelf. "This is Penelope. She's yours until Monday." The size of a real baby, Penelope has arms and legs made of tinted squeezable plastic, wears a diaper and a pair of pajamas, and wide brown eyes grace her serene face. A swirl of raised plastic on her forehead, like a tiny cinnamon bun, represents a wisp of hair. Ms. Robinson puts her in my arms, then hands me a set of five square plastic keys that are to be used to soothe her.

One says "Feed." The next says "Burp." Another says "Attention." The fourth says "Sleep." The last says "Change." She turns the baby over. On Penelope's back is a hard plastic inset that resembles the controls for a video game, with a slot where I am to insert the plastic keys. Ms. Robinson explains that Penelope will cry every three to four hours, including during the night. I will need to figure out what's wrong, and insert the proper key to quiet her. If I choose the wrong one, she will keep crying. Once the key is inserted, it must be held for fifteen minutes, which would represent about the amount of time it would take to feed, change, or pay attention to the baby.

Ms. Robinson signs Penelope out to me. "If you're successful with Penelope, you can possibly end up with a C."

"Thank you, Ms. Robinson." I realize she has done me a huge favor. In spite of the zero, which I have to admit, I earned. Ms. Robinson has been unbelievably kind to me.

She looks at Ziggy I, II, III, and IV. "Why don't you take them all home? Some of this flour may still be good. Does anyone at your house like to bake?"

CHAPTER THIRTEEN

AND SO, I waddle down the hall to my locker at a snail's pace, struggling with Penelope and twenty pounds of flour.

I hate Harrison. I hate him! Sure, maybe I ignored him. I didn't like him back. I wasn't exactly *nice* to him. But I wasn't *mean* to him. I didn't *deliberately* do anything to him. I defended him when he was bullied! Why would he do this to me?

At that moment, Ziggy II slips from my arms, lands with a *thunk*, and splits open. Puffs of flour spill across the floor, like ground fog on a mountain road, and skid over the shiny linoleum. I dump all the Ziggys and Penelope just outside the computer room door. Why the heck didn't I ask Ms. Robinson for a bag? On my knees, I try to scoop the flour back into the broken bag.

Pretty soon I've got flour up to my elbows, all over the front of my shirt, caking my jeans. I can only guess it's on my face and in my hair. And still there's more on the floor. It's multiplying.

I sneeze.

The computer room is only a few feet away. Even though

the door is closed and the sign says, "Mr. Joya will be back in ten minutes," I figure I can duck in there and grab a trash can to scoop up all the flour. I scurry inside with Penelope, turn on the lights, and reach for one of the trash cans.

At that moment, a jarring cry erupts.

My heart beats once, very hard, so hard my chest hurts.

What was that? It blares in my ear. The school fire alarm again?

Oh! God, it's Penelope.

With trembling hands, I get out the ring of square plastic keys. Which is it? I try "Feed." Nope. Not that one. Penelope's cry gets louder. She sounds like a sick goat.

Is it "Burp?" My hands shake so much I drop the keys. Gingerly I pick them up, and try "Burp." Nope.

She winds up to a good yowl now, and it starts to echo around the computer room walls, sounding more like a sick moose.

Can I rip out her batteries?

I jam the square "Attention" key into her back. And suddenly, she is silent.

I stand in the middle of the computer room, relief washing over me, her crying still echoing inside my head. I'm supposed to hold the key for fifteen minutes. My underarms are wet.

Footsteps sound behind me. I gasp and whirl around.

Andy!

We both jump, and in the resulting arm bobble, I drop Penelope. The key falls out, and she starts crying again.

"What are you doing in the computer lab?" Andy's eyes are so wide you'd think he saw an alien.

"It's a long story. I came in here to get a trash can so I can pick up the flour I spilled in the hall." I grab Penelope from the floor, and start jamming the keys in her back again. She finally responds to the same key again—"Attention." There is sudden quiet. I blow my bangs off my forehead. I start to ask Andy why he ghosted me, but then he speaks first.

"So," Andy says slowly, "you're not the pranker, right?"

I drop my jaw. "Of course not, Andy! How could you think that?"

He shrugs. "Just making sure. I didn't really think so."

"So...uh...what are *you* doing here?"

Andy hesitates. "Oh, nothing." His eyes stray to a corner of the room, then he seems to make a decision. "Okay. I'm putting a camera in here to see if I can catch the kids doing this. Quick, can you help me? Before Mr. Joya gets back?"

Once again I am drawn into the vortex of his charisma. For a long second I am undecided, thinking about the agony I've been through ever since I went to Billy Z's. Then, I decide. "What do you want me to do?"

"I'm going to stand on a table and tape this camera on top of the loudspeaker. Hand the camera up to me."

He pulls a roll of duct tape from his pocket, then hands me a small video camera before scrambling up onto the computer table closest to the loudspeaker. He pulls a few pieces of tape and sticks them to the front of his shirt. "Okay, hand it up," he says.

I hand him the camera and watch, frozen, as he tapes the camera flat on top of the loudspeaker where it can barely be seen. He presses "Record" and the red light flicks on.

"Now if anybody comes in here they'll be recorded," he says. "Thank you, dizzy Lizzy!" He jumps down, and squeezes my hand. "We're going to catch these jokers. Come on, let's vamoose." He hurries out of the computer room.

I grab the trash can for my flour babies, feeling excited. Andy isn't the pranker. He's trying to find out who the pranker is. And I helped him. I realize that when he first hit record the camera was on me, but it should be obvious that I wasn't doing anything.

"What are you doing in here?"

I whirl around toward the voice.

It's Mr. Joya.

"Oh, I...I dropped my flour baby and came in here to find a trash can."

Mr. Joya glances over at the bank of computers. Then he glances at me, covered in flour, and my face, which must look guilty. "Maybe you need to tell that story to the principal. Let's go."

———

I sit in the conference room behind the principal's office with Mrs. J. She empties the contents of my purse onto the conference room table and along with the pens, and Jolly Ranchers, out rolls the marker I've been using to draw Ziggy's face. As I raise my eyes from the marker, I meet Mrs. J's.

Mr. Joya, when I saw him, had just left Ms. Robinson's classroom where she had discovered that several of the grades for ninth grade Health, including mine, had been mysteriously changed. Mrs. J's gaze bores into mine without mercy. I try to take a breath but my chest feels like it's caught in a vise.

Without speaking, she crosses her arms over her chest. The fluorescent light in the ceiling flickers, making it feel like a surreal movie scene. Someone must have heated up some Chef Boyardee Ravioli in the microwave across the hall for an early lunch because I can smell it.

The custodian was called to take care of the remains of Ziggy II. I was allowed to put Ziggy I, III, and IV in my locker. Penelope sits in my lap. Since she just cried a few minutes ago, maybe I'm safe for a while.

"So, Elizabeth." Mrs. J picks up a pen and opens my school file. "Why don't you tell me what you were doing in the computer lab just now."

"I dropped my flour baby while I was walking by and flour went all over the hall, and I went in to get a trash can to try to clean it up." I frown. Somehow I have to tell her that what I said on the website last night about Andy was wrong.

She sits back in her chair, and crosses her legs. Her iron gray hair is like a helmet. Mrs. J is as stern as I've ever seen her. "Just to get a trash can."

"Yes, ma'am." I rub my slightly shaking finger over the raised plastic curl on Penelope's forehead. I remember that nursery rhyme, *Once there was a girl...who had a little curl, right in the middle of her forehead. When she was good, she was very, very good...and when she was bad she was horrid.*

"And then what happened?"

I meet her eyes. I make a point to look and sound earnest, based on the conversation with Dad about *The Importance of Being Earnest.* I tell her about everything, including taping the camera to the loudspeaker with Andy.

"So there's a video camera in the computer room recording right now?"

"Yes, ma'am."

"We'll have to talk with Andy about that."

"He wasn't doing anything bad! He's trying to catch the pranker!"

When I'm finished, Mrs. J closes my file. "Will we find your fingerprints on the keyboard of one of the computers in the computer lab?

"No, ma'am."

"Do you want to reconsider your answer? Five people's grades had been changed to As and yours was one of them.

Changing teachers' home pages and triggering fake fire drills is one kind of prank. Changing grades is another entirely."

My eyes sting. I'm not going to cry. "No, ma'am. I did not touch any of the computers."

"You did not change any of the grades for the ninth grade Health class?"

"No, ma'am." My mind races.

I glance at the clock on the wall above the credenza. It's 11:00. Time for changes of classes and everyone to go to Health class. The second hand does not sweep smoothly around the edge. It inches along and at one point it seems to get stuck, trembling and straining to advance. My head feels like it's going to explode.

"You should know, Elizabeth, that another student has anonymously turned in your name as a possible suspect."

"What?" The blood drains out of my face. My whole body feels frozen.

"Maybe you'd like to reconsider what you've said?"

I'm not guilty of anything! Who would have turned my name in other than Harrison? I blink at her. "Was it Harrison?"

"I'm sorry, Elizabeth, the person turned you in anonymously so I cannot reveal the name."

"Maybe Harrison turned me in, Mrs. J, because he's mad at me."

She studies me in silence. She writes a few notes. "Why is he mad at you?"

I begin to understand why people sometimes confess to things they haven't done. I'm so flustered by her questions. "I think he has a crush on me and I've been kind of mean to him and I—I think I hurt him. I think he's trying to get me back."

"I see." Her face gives nothing away. She writes a few more notes. "Is there any other information that you might be able to share with me?"

A little whisper in my ear says to come clean about everything.

So I tell her about taking the memory card to Billy Z. I tell her about using the website to report Andy last night. "But now I know Andy didn't do it. The memory card just has the interview with you on it, that's all. The anonymous person who turned Andy in was me, and I really didn't have any proof. He isn't the pranker," I repeat. "He's trying to catch the pranker."

"Do you know that for a fact? Did you look at the memory card? Could it have had anything else on it?" Mrs. J's eyes narrow and she cocks her head at me.

"I didn't look at it. I didn't actually know what was on it until the broadcast today."

"I see. That's odd, isn't it? Not being curious enough to look at it."

My eyes wander around the room. Is that a sign of guilt? I try looking right at her, but can't seem to hold her gaze. My face feels like it's on the verge of collapsing into hysterical sobbing. This is such a nightmare. I wish I could wake up.

The second hand leaps forward. A roaring fills my head.

Mrs. J scoots her chair closer to the conference table and drums her pen on the surface a few times, then leans her face close to mine. "I have heard," she says, "that this hasn't been a good week for you. You had to go to detention for disruptive behavior—for the first time since you've been a Lakeside student—and Ms. Robinson says you lied about an assignment for her class. She said you seemed extremely worried about not getting an A. Plus, turning Andy in could have been a way of deflecting suspicion from yourself. I have also heard from Officer Egan that he found you out riding your bike in the middle of the night last night."

Gosh, I sound like I could really be guilty. I know I should answer but I'm speechless.

"This is uncharacteristic behavior for you," Mrs. J goes on. "Normally you are an excellent student who gets her work done and participates in a number of school activities. Miss Bebe has told me that this week for the first time you're not allowed to participate in the cheerleading competition."

Mrs. J blinks very slowly. I never noticed before that she has blue eyes like icebergs.

"Yes." I can hardly talk now. Does she believe me? It's weird to be telling the absolute truth and feel like, no matter what I did, Mrs. J won't believe me.

I think about how I wondered about all those kids in detention, like Carrie Raznik, and Lance Spock, and how I gossiped with the other cheerleaders about how it might be Harrison, and how I even suspected Andy (Andy!) of doing this. How I even turned him in. And now it's come full circle and I am a suspect myself.

"You may return to class at this time. However, we may be calling your parents about a possible suspension."

"Suspension?" My mouth is so dry I can hardly say the word.

CHAPTER FOURTEEN

MY KNEES SHAKE as Penelope and I head down the hall to Ms. Robinson's class, trying to dust the flour off my clothes as I walk. My face heats up.

Mom is going to be *so* mad at me. Dad, too. Every time I imagine the disappointment on their faces when they find out, hot tears spring to my eyes. When I think about the things I've done this week—the handsprings on the soccer field, lying about the flour babies, going to detention, turning Andy in, riding to Billy Z's house in the middle of the night—it's stuff I've never done before, never would have dreamed of doing before. Maybe I really have been invaded by a pod person, like Ryan said.

I turn the corner and gasp when I see Harrison, with a pink hall pass in his hand.

"Harrison!" I pull Penelope close to my body, still holding the key firmly in her back. "Why did you take my flour babies? And why did you turn them into Ms. Robinson? Why didn't you give them back?"

"I didn't take them!"

"You did!"

Harrison can't hold my eyes any longer. He looks at a spot on the floor. "Okay, I took the second one during Biology. I found the first one by the water fountain."

I lick my dry lips. "Why would you do that? Why didn't you give them back to me?"

"Why should I do anything nice for you? What have you ever done for me, except ignore me? Except laugh and run away from me? I thought you were different from everyone else, but you're not, you're just the same!" His eyes narrow and tears tremble on his lower eyelids. He brushes roughly past me and down the hall.

I let out my breath slowly. So I did actually lose two flour babies. Harrison took one. It was because I ignored him. But I didn't want attention from him. And shouldn't I be allowed to feel that way?

I square my shoulders and head to Health class.

I hand Ms. Robinson my pink excused tardy slip, slide into my chair as unobtrusively as possible, and lay Penelope across my lap. Mr. Joya has been able to restore the computer screens to the SmartBoard, so the class is watching a movie about a teen mom. Half the students rest their heads on their desks in the semi-dark, and no one seems to have noticed that I wasn't there. On a screen at the front of the room, a baby hiccups and spits yellow stuff on her teenage mother's shirt. Then the baby wraps little wet fingers in the girl's hair and pulls. Ow! It reminds me of seeing Casey in the restaurant.

Everyone has turned in their flour babies and they are lined up on Ms. Robinson's work table. Andy's baseball baby. Carrie Raznik's Freddy Krueger. Michael Phelps. Tanya's cubist Woman. Kelly's Marie Curie. Marisa's anime girl. Harrison's Einstein. All those babies, beat-up, dirty, and worn after being lugged around for a week. I'm embarrassed to be carrying Penelope now, since everyone has turned theirs in.

But nobody seems to notice that, either.

Andy turns around and whispers, "What happened?" His face is unreadable in the semi-darkness.

I jump. So, he hasn't found out about anything yet. He hasn't heard that I turned him in. That I told about the camera. That I'm a suspect. He's being nice to me. Still, I turn away. I feel so guilty, I can't face him.

And I still want to know why he ghosted me.

I think about the tingly stream of energy I'd been feeling from him for this past week. For a while, and even today in the computer room, I believed he really cared about me. But now I think maybe he never did. And what would he think now, if he knew that I turned him in last night?

My head is swirling with these chaotic thoughts when, once again, the fire bell clangs. Once again, we all jump.

"Mr. Joya said once we changed our passwords this would be fixed," says Ms. Robinson. "So I don't know what's going on. But, ladies and gentlemen, even though we know this is a prank, we're still required to follow our evacuation procedure. Please line up and proceed quietly and quickly to the soccer field. There should be no talking."

Moans, sighs, and groans erupt. I grab Penelope and head for the door. I can feel Andy right behind me—that vortex force of his energy bearing down.

"Lizzy. Pretty Tin Lizzy. Want me to sing some Bon Iver or John Mayer? So, hey, why aren't you talking to me?"

He definitely doesn't know I turned him in. Or that I told about the camera. I draw Penelope closer and keep walking down the hall.

He skips alongside, just like he did at the beginning of the week. "Hey, what's up with you, Busy Tin Lizzy? Too busy for the dance tonight?"

"Leave me alone, Andy." I grip Penelope close against my rib cage, so tight I worry that she'll start to cry.

"Lizzy." He drops the act, or changes to a new act. The Earnest Reporter. "Seriously, what's wrong?"

I head down the stairs. "I just got interviewed by Mrs. J. They think I'm an actual suspect. They're going to call my parents. I've been so stupid." I stop on the stair landing, and am finally able to look up at him. "I did so many things, all because you asked me to. Things that got me into trouble. And you never even answered my text after I rode over to Billy Z's in the middle of the night!"

He holds up one hand as if being sworn in to give testimony in a court of law. "That's not my fault! My dad took my phone when he found out I was suspended!" His emerald eyes are wide, his narrow face suffused with...earnestness.

From here I can look out the window at the soccer field and see everyone spilling out there, walking in lines like colorful ants. Everyone's giddy since we know it's a prank. Should I believe him? "So your dad took your phone."

He leans in. "You have to believe me, Lizzy."

He takes my hand. I start to pull away and then I let myself feel his palm next to mine.

People file past and Ms. Robinson's nose practically comes between us. "Evacuate!"

I push past him, hugging Penelope close. I follow the crowd down the hall and find myself out on the soccer field beside Marisa. A damp breeze makes the hairs on my arms stand on end. We sit cross-legged in the grass, watching the stragglers come out of the building. People around us talk, text, or lie back and stare at a moody, purplish sky. Today it's overcast and drizzling. We huddle silently in the gloom, putting our jackets on the ground to avoid sitting on the damp grass. The air feels electric, like it's supercharged with ions.

Andy sits by himself a few yards away, looking glum. Every now and then he scowls over at me.

"Where were you?" Marisa flips her dark hair behind her shoulder, then picks through the grass, looking for four-leaf clovers.

"Oh, it was nothing, I was talking to Andy."

"I thought you liked him."

"That was before."

"He's staring at you." When I don't answer, she adds, "Are you okay?" She squints at me, shading her eyes with her hand.

I don't want to tell Marisa about being questioned by Mrs. J. I don't want anyone to know. I still feel shell-shocked from the whole thing. I can't tell her about what I did for Andy or about turning him in or even why I'm mad at him. I know it wasn't him, but I'm still so angry. "Yeah, this whole fire drill thing is just getting old, that's all."

"I know. I wish they'd catch whoever it is."

"Are you still going to Florida for spring break?"

"Yeah, I guess I'm going to miss a day of school. Maybe even two."

The officers and firefighters meander out of the school and climb back into their vehicles under the threatening sky.

"Sooo...what happened with Andy? You're not going to hang out at the dance with him tonight?" Marisa continues her clover search.

"I don't know." My brain buzzes with all the confusing thoughts and feelings about him. I feel a tingling along my neckline, thinking that he's watching me. "He ghosted me. He stopped texting me." I finally decide to tell Marisa part of the truth. "And he just told me his dad took his phone because he was suspended for doing that interview inside the school when we were supposed to be evacuated."

"So you don't believe him?" Marisa asks.

"Well, even if his dad did take his phone, he still could've borrowed someone else's, just to send me a text, couldn't he?"

"I guess," Marisa says. "But guys are different, Lizzy." She starts laughing. "A lot of times they can't think of anything to say. Sometimes Cody goes whole days without texting me. I don't get mad at him for it."

I want to tell Marisa that she doesn't understand, but then I'd have to tell her everything. I want to sweep those thoughts away. I never want to think about Andy again. Suddenly, I spot a clover with four lucky leaves. I snap its slender stalk, aware that he's probably still watching, and hand it to her. "Found one!"

Marisa twirls it, and her eyes grow serious as she examines each leaf. "You found one!" She holds it out to me. "Make a wish."

"You make one. I found it for you."

She regards me soberly, and then holds the clover between us. "We'll both make a wish."

We share the stalk, each touching it with only the edge of our thumb and index finger. I squeeze my eyes shut, wondering how to choose from the many wishes I could make. I wish...Chief Ballou wouldn't call my parents? I wish...I hadn't turned Andy in? I wish...Andy was earnest? I wish...I could go to the dance tonight? I open my eyes and catch Marisa staring at me, smiling.

"I bet I know what you wished."

I give her a tight smile. What she said sort of changed my mind. Maybe, if Andy texts me again about the dance, I'll say yes.

"Don't tell me, or it won't come true." She gives my arm a little pinch.

"What did you wish?" I ask her.

"Can't tell."

I pinch her back and we laugh.

"Attention students." Mrs. J's voice booms across the soccer field just like on game days. "I have an announcement to make. We have identified the persons doing the pranks."

We jump to our feet and cheer.

"You may return to your classrooms. Miracle of miracles, some instruction may take place today. Please also give our valiant firefighters and police officers a round of applause for their hard work."

We clap wildly.

"And you can thank some of your fellow students for their help apprehending these prankers."

I can hardly believe my ears. She means Andy and me! I guess she can't tell anyone who we are but even so everyone begins to cheer. I try to steal a glance at Andy, but he isn't sitting in the same place anymore. The sounds of the cheers reverberate around us.

Ms. Robinson and Mr. Waggoner, standing together, have looks of amazement on their faces.

Marisa and I stand and knock the grass from the seats of our jeans.

My feeling of well-being is short-lived, though. As we file across the field, thunder rumbles and large raindrops begin to plop onto us, at first slowly, then harder. Within moments, a cold and punishing spring rain pelts us.

And then, out of nowhere, there's a huge reverberating BOOM!

A bomb, a bomb has gone off, I think.

My body tenses. My heart pounds. Where did it come from?

Now there are pops and smaller booms. *Gunfire*. Oh. No.

Everyone is screaming and running, but we can't tell where

the sounds are coming from. Some people freeze, and others run in every direction.

I am screaming, too.

Then there's a long burst of popping sounds. *A machine gun. I don't want to die.*

Then, brilliant white sparks shoot from the dumpster on the other side of the soccer field.

Still screaming, people are running in all directions—away from the Dumpster, toward the parking lot, toward the woods. Some students race to their cars, get inside and duck down.

In the next moment, with a loud cracking sound, the contents of the dumpster ignite and flames lick the sky.

The screaming fills my ears. It's complete mayhem. I'm so scared my heart is in my throat and I'm pushed along with the crowd running for the front door. I grab Marisa's hand. The rain pelts us like a spring hail storm. The teachers yell, "No running!" But no one listens, and we push our way toward the doors. The teachers yell again, but it's no use. Someone stomps my foot just as another person shoves me from behind, knocking the breath out of me. Sharp elbows stab my ribs.

Marisa's hand slips away and she screams my name as she falls. The crowd closes around her.

"Marisa!" I push against the bodies closing in on me, leaning down to reach for her. I'm pummeled from all sides as I'm reaching, but I somehow grasp her fingers. My shoulder pops as I try to pull her up, as if it's been dislocated. Breathless, my skin slick with rain and sweat, I pull Marisa to her feet.

She crashes against me and I trip on the curb, dropping Penelope. One of her batteries falls out and rolls across the sidewalk. I fumble between people's legs, trying to pick it up.

Someone steps right on my hand as my fingers close around the battery. I fall to the ground, twisting my arm. Someone else steps on my hair and I hear ripping as some of it pulls out.

I curl into a ball. Hold Penelope and the battery tight to my chest.

Beside me, I hear someone groan. It's Chelsea, the girl who hangs with the Goths, on the ground beside me. People step on her as they run by.

"Chelsea!" I fight my way over through the pouring rain. "Come on, we'll get up together. On three." I'm panting and dodging feet. Someone's foot pounds my rib. "One. Two. Three!"

To help Chelsea, I have to leave Penelope behind. I drop the doll, and heave myself to my knees, pulling Chelsea with me. I grasp her around her waist, shouting and shoving people out of the way. "Now, up!" I struggle to my feet, dragging her with me.

"I'm bleeding!" she yells at me.

"It's okay, it's okay," I keep saying, because it's all I can think to say. I remember how she cried about her cat, and I see that scared girl is still there inside.

Holding tight to Chelsea, I spot a covered bench by the school entrance that's outside the stampede. I steer her in that direction, out of the pull of the crowd. At last we reach the bench and collapse onto it. The rain is coming down sideways in sheets.

Flames continue to billow out of the Dumpster. The firefighters are spraying it with water from their hoses. Thank god they were already here because of the alarm. My heart beats double-time.

Chelsea must have cut her arm badly because it's bleeding a lot. I remember Dad telling me about tourniquets being part of Red Cross training. I feel amazingly calm. What do I have that I could use as a tourniquet?

My sock. I rip it off, along with my shoe, in one motion, and tie it tight around her arm. "Ok, I've put on a tourniquet, you're going to be ok. Take some deep breaths."

"Lizzy!" someone yells. I feel wet arms reach around both Chelsea and me. That person feels strong and caring. Is it Ryan? Andy? I look up.

It's Ms. Robinson. "Girls, are you all right? I was afraid you were getting trampled." She holds us tight, her arms over our shoulders. "Are you hurt?"

I stretch my fingers, and rub my scalp where the hair got pulled out. I feel like I can't talk, but whisper, "I think I'm okay. But Chelsea's arm is hurt."

"We'll get her to the nurse. Looks like you did a good job with the tourniquet, Lizzy," Ms. Robinson says. She leads us through the rain toward the school entrance. The students are huddled inside now. I'm looking everywhere for Ryan, and finally spot him with his AP English class. He's been looking for me, too, and he waves at me across the parking lot with relief.

Ms. Robinson stops, scoops something up and hands it to me. It's Penelope. "Here. When you're taking care of a real person, you're excused for losing a mechanical doll."

I hold Penelope tight against my chest, to keep from crying. By the time Ms. Robinson guides us into the school and takes Chelsea to find the nurse, I've replaced Penelope's battery with shaking hands.

I don't even bother to look for Andy. I will my heart not to beat so fast, to slow down, but I have no control over it. I open and close the fingers of my bruised hand. My one foot feels weird without a sock, and I limp toward a corner of the room, away from the crowd.

———

Just as we file back into our classroom, all of us dripping wet, our clothes sticking to us, the static of Mrs. J's voice spurts over the loudspeaker. "Attention students. Someone set off a firecracker in the soccer field dumpster. The firefighters have extinguished the fire. Although we do not yet know who set off the firecracker, we have identified those who have been doing the other pranks. Effective immediately, the students who did set off the alarms will be expelled from our school system."

I quickly glance around the room and catch my breath. Andy isn't here.

Then, like the rippling of dominoes, students in our classroom and those all down the hall burst into enthusiastic and spontaneous applause. There's chattering all around me as everyone guesses who the culprit is, who will be expelled, and what will happen next.

A few people blurt, "Who was it?"

Someone murmurs, "Didn't you hear?"

Almost as though she's heard, Ms. J says, "We lost valuable teaching time and wasted the time of our valiant police and fire personnel. We will be losing the first two days of our spring break this year to make up the time we have lost."

I look around the classroom. Andy is still not back. My hand throbs. The loudspeaker goes silent now.

"My goodness," says Ms. Robinson. "That is the best news I've heard all semester. All's well that ends well. There is not enough time during the rest of the period today for the quiz on the flour baby unit, so we'll have the quiz on Monday. You may use your time for the rest of the period to review your notes." With a flourish, she turns off the SmartBoard. "And I don't know about you folks, but I've had enough excitement this week to last my entire lifetime." She strides to the back of the room and collapses at her desk.

A few students pull out their phones and start texting and she watches them with glazed eyes, without even telling them to stop. After staring into space for a few seconds, she pulls out a stack of papers to grade.

People continue to buzz and gossip about who the prankers might be. I hear Andy's name. I hear other names.

Ms. Robinson grades her papers as if she is deaf, as if having to tell us to be quiet now, after all that has happened, is simply more than she can bear. I use the time to try to review Harrison's notes, though I can't seem to get my heart to slow down to normal.

Once the bell rings, I head with Marisa to lunch, though I have no appetite. The back of my hand has developed a greenish bruise and my scalp hurts. I wonder how Chelsea is doing. I wish I could go home and curl up on my bed.

"Didn't it sound like it was more than one person?" Marisa says. "Eventually we'll figure it out because they won't be at school. And there'll be rumors," she adds.

I sit quietly, stunned. Someone is already missing.

———

By the time we get to Biology, Harrison isn't here. Quite a few people in our class aren't here, in fact.

"I told you Harrison was a prime suspect," Kelly says, showing me her graph. "He was one of the major people on my grid. If he's not back on Monday, I guess we'll know for sure."

I shrug. I don't say anything to Kelly about what happened with Harrison in the hall this morning. I have to clear my mind for the dissection test. I have to calm down from that firecracker. I have to conquer my nausea from the smell of the formaldehyde. I have to concentrate. I have to force myself to stop thinking about Andy.

"Mrs. Cruz, do we still have to take the test, even with all the pranks?" asks Sanjay.

I am hoping Mrs. Cruz says no because I know I haven't studied enough.

"Indeed you do," says Mrs. Cruz, her brown eyes flashing. "April Fools' week is officially over."

Mrs. Cruz has placed four of the fetal pigs at stations in the room, each decorated with twenty pins with numbered flags. We move from one pig to the next, identifying their body parts.

It's one of the hardest tests I've ever taken. Harrison's notes helped, but forgetting to study last night was a huge mistake. I keep getting the various systems mixed up, especially the circulatory system. As much as I love the beautiful way the organs fit snugly into the body cavity, the elegant way each organ works together with the others to maintain life, the seamless way the arteries thread their way from our hearts to the rest of our body, as amazed as I am by the brilliant design and reliability of the physical body—I am screwed because I haven't gotten it all memorized.

I am still struggling with the circulatory system when I see Kelly sign her test paper and hand it to Mrs. Cruz with a hopeful smile.

"How do you think you did, Kelly?" she asks. "Would you like me to grade it right now?

Kelly nods, and Mrs. Cruz gets a red pen from her desk and quickly scans down the answers, touching the point of the pen to the paper in her methodical way. She reaches the end of the page without any Xs. Then she turns to the back.

She reaches the end of the back page and then turns the sheet back over. In her neat handwriting, she carefully writes "100" in the upper right hand corner of the page. She looks up at Kelly, smiles, and then places her paper in the desk drawer.

Kelly has made a hundred. That means there will be no curve. I feel the heat of the flush on my cheeks, but when Kelly looks over at me I force myself to smile and give her a thumbs up.

I am one of the last to turn in my paper but no matter how

long I sit there and think, the information just isn't in my brain. While I should have been studying last night I was riding my bike to Billy Z's and being escorted home by Officer Egan. I realize that if there were anything I wanted more than Andy, it is a one hundred from Mrs. Cruz. And I'm not going to get it.

"Would you like me to grade it now, Lizzy?" Mrs. Cruz asks when I hand her my paper.

I almost say "No, thanks," but then I nod.

She puts a few Xs on the front page, turns to the back, and then there's a shower of them beside the circulatory system.

"Sixty-two," she says, circling the number at the top corner.

An F! I got an F! That's never happened before. This is the worst week of my life. What am I going to do? I will never be allowed to go to the freshman dance now.

"You can do better, Lizzy," Mrs. Cruz says.

"I know," I say. All I want is to get out of this classroom.

"Next time," she adds, "you will." She gives me a hard stare.

———

When school lets out this afternoon, it's crazier than usual. I trudge outside, still wearing only one sock, struggling to keep Penelope and three bags of flour in my arms. It's a huge relief to have this awful week over with. There's cheerleading practice today, but since I forgot my permission slip I'm not in the competition. So I'm in the midst of students waiting beside the parking lot for rides. In the melee of hugs, squeals, and erratic milling, someone sings "Skinny Love" by Bon Iver at the top of their lungs, reminding me of the first time I talked to Andy.

Goose bumps prickle slowly over my scalp.

Ryan will be the last to pick me up, so I wander to the end of the line. I line up Ziggy I, III, and IV on the curb. From here I can stand on my tiptoes and see the baseball field, where puffs of reddish dust swirl behind the players as they round the bases. The figures are too small for me to tell if Andy is out there or not. I try to see if I can recognize the way he runs, since I've been studying the way he moves all week and have it memorized. But I can't see anybody who looks like him.

Has he been suspended? Maybe I will be able to find out from Marisa after the dance tonight. If things had been different, tonight I might be standing next to him by the punch bowl or slow dancing with my cheek buried in his skinny chest, listening to his heart.

How giddy everyone seems.

When I turn back toward the front of the school, I see Harrison and his parents coming out of the front door. His dad has his arm over Harrison's shoulder as they head toward the parking lot. They have serious expressions on their faces. As they're climbing into a green Volvo, I think about what Dad would want me to do, and I give a half-hearted wave. But Harrison doesn't look at me or respond. He just gets in the car and the family drives away.

Finally, when practically the only people left outside Lakeside High are Ziggy I, III, IV, and me, the Millennium Falcon coasts to a stop at the curb. I lean down to pick up Penelope and the Ziggys as Ryan peers over the passenger seat and out the window. "Penelope and the Ziggy Flour Babies," I say. "I'm starting a girl band."

Ryan laughs.

I get in the car without looking back at the baseball field.

CHAPTER FIFTEEN

ANY MINUTE, Mom is due home from her new job. Dad called a few minutes ago from work, and he's on his way home, too. If I make cookies for Mom and Dad, maybe they will go easy on me with the zero in Health and the F in Mrs. Cruz's class.

Who am I kidding?

But Andy did mention the dance today. So there's still a chance I could see him there and work this thing out. Isn't there? Maybe he has a good explanation for everything he's done. Maybe I've been too hard on him. Misjudged him.

Am I being completely crazy to hope?

The oven has preheated and I only ate two tablespoons of the raw cookie dough so I have enough left to arrange the gooey blobs two inches apart on the cookie sheet.

I opened Ziggy III to make the cookies and she sits on the counter, next to Ziggy I and IV, misshapen and smaller, with her head folded down. Penelope is propped on one of the high-backed chairs we use to sit at the counter. On the way home, I tried to tell Ryan about being interviewed about the pranks and getting trampled, and not seeing Andy for the rest of the day, but Penelope started wailing. While I fumbled, trying to insert the correct key, Ryan started yelling, "Crazy, this is driving me!"

"You? What about me?" I yelled back. "This has been the worst week of my life!"

After I finally found "Burp," and she stopped crying, Ryan asked, "Do you still think Andy might be involved?"

I leaned against the car door, holding Penelope's key in place. "No, I'm sure he's not the pranker." I told him about running into Andy in the computer room and helping him with the camera.

"Awesome that you helped," Ryan said.

Now, just as the oven buzzer goes off, Mom bursts through the door, breathless. "Lizzy, that smells wonderful! I got a group email from your principal. Wow, what a day you and Ryan must have had." She drops her purse and keys on the kitchen table and gives me a tight hug. She hasn't hugged me in a week, and the tears prick again when I feel her close. "Thank goodness they caught those kids!" She runs her hand through her dark, newly-dyed hair. "What a relief! And good for them for expelling those kids. Do you know who they are?"

"Nope. Hey, you got your hair done. It looks good, Mom."

Mom grins. "Yes—right after work!"

The back door opens and Dad steps into the kitchen in his work suit. "I smell cookies!" he says. "I've been waiting for this all week!" He glances at Mom's hair. "You look nice, Ellen."

Mom puts her hand on her hip and cocks her head, fluffs her hair, and smiles. "Why, thank you, Wayne."

"How was the first day?" Dad asks.

A funny look crosses Mom's face and she glances away. "I poked a hole in the wall."

"With the forklift?" Dad slaps his forehead and I cover my mouth.

"Well, I was trying to load this container, and I just didn't have a good idea how far the metal bars were out in front of me and...well, it wasn't a very big hole."

"Did you get fired?"

Mom shakes her head. "Mr. Sebastiano said everyone does it once." She shrugs. "Nobody's perfect." Then she lines up Ziggy I, III, and IV and stares at their faces. "Lizzy, what are all of these bags of flour doing on the counter?"

"Oh, those are my flour babies." I slide the spatula under the cookies and they pop smoothly off the cookie sheet and onto the platter. They are steaming and still gooey in the middle. I timed them perfectly. We'll all eat cookies, and maybe everything will be okay. "Speaking of not being perfect, I need to tell you both about my week."

"Why are there three flour babies?" Dad says, as he takes a hot cookie and blows on it. "I thought you only needed one."

At that moment Ryan comes downstairs, blithely humming the theme from *Mission: Impossible.*

"Yes, Lizzy, why are there three of them?" Mom echoes.

"Extra credit?" Ryan suggests. He glances at me, resumes his humming, much louder, and takes four cookies. "Dum-tum, dee-dee, dum-tum, dee-dee, dum-tum, dee-dee, dum-tum, dee-dee! Doodleoo! Doodleoo!" He starts back up the stairs but then comes back to the counter. With a slow smile, he leans over and takes another cookie.

"Another cookie, anybody?" I say.

Mom skewers me with her eyes.

"I ...made a few mistakes this week. Mom, as much as I hate admitting this, you were right, I did lose my flour baby. In fact, I lost three of them. So. There they are." I take a very deep, cleansing breath. I'm admitting it. I'm admitting everything.

Mom chews her cookie more slowly, as if it suddenly doesn't taste so good. "This is news to me."

Ryan pushes off the counter and swipes a few more cookies. "Alrighty then, see you guys later." He starts across to the stairs.

"Ryan?" I yell. "You can't leave me!"

"Who is this little doll sitting here on the counter, Lizzy?" Dad asks.

"That's Penelope," I say.

"Penelope." Mom repeats. "Lizzy?" A warning voice. "Is this just another example of you being irresponsible?"

I look at Mom and Dad and something breaks in me and I completely lose it. "This is not all my fault!" I yell.

"Lizzy, control yourself," Dad says.

"I'm not going to control myself! I didn't lose all of my flour babies! Someone was taking them! This has been the worst week of my life. You all don't understand that I'm under a lot of pressure. Just like you said, Mom, nobody's perfect!" I am completely out of breath and my temples are throbbing with anger.

"Lizzy, it's so unlike you to lose your temper like this," says Dad.

I burst into tears.

———

Later, I sit on my bed with the bedclothes all rumpled as hot tears plop onto the face of my cell phone.

Mom and Dad are deciding on my punishment. They say it was dishonest of me to go get new flour babies after losing them.

They're right.

They point out that was the POINT of the Health unit. Dad says he doesn't care if there were a hundred prank fire drills this week. And Mom says she doesn't care that Harrison was stealing my flour babies; I still tried to conceal the fact that they were gone.

I can't disagree.

My head is throbbing so intensely that I look it up on *Five Minute Med Consult*, and I think it's entirely possible that I am having an aneurysm.

I hear a knock on my bedroom door. "What?" I pull the covers over Penelope and me.

Dad and Mom both come in and softly close the door.

"Lizzy," Dad says.

"What?" My lips are swollen from crying and I feel like I can hardly talk. It's probably a good thing I can't go to the dance because I look like I have a fat lip.

Mom sits at my desk and Dad perches awkwardly on the foot of my bed. He doesn't come in my room often. His eyes scan the wadded jeans and tops scattered on the floor. For a moment, he lightly lays his palm on the back of my head. "I know that boy was taking the flour babies. But you lied. Both to us, and to your teachers. It's not the fact that you were forgetful that's the problem—it's the fact that you lied."

"I know, Dad. I just...felt so stupid about being forgetful, I didn't want to get in trouble, so I tried to cover it up." The shame creeps over me again, like a hot mud bath.

"Lizzy, some of the world's most creative and productive people have been absentminded. I think a lot of times you forget everyday tasks because you're thinking about the more important things in life," Mom finishes.

"You do?" I stare at Mom, then at Dad.

"Yes, we do." Dad smiles at me.

A weight lifts from my shoulders. I blink. And in that blink, suddenly, everything I see seems different.

"You want to be a doctor, Lizzy, I have no doubt that you can do it if you put your mind to it. Not only are you smart, you're kind and caring. And that's the type of people we need as doctors," Dad says.

"I used my sock as a tourniquet today to help a girl whose arm was bleeding after she fell in the parking lot."

"That was quick thinking, " Mom says. "Now, that doesn't mean you shouldn't try to develop systems for yourself to help you remember things. Dad uses a couple of reminder apps on his phone. I make lists. Try some different tactics. But I don't want you ever again to lie to cover it up. Understand?"

I nod.

"So you'll be grounded for two weeks," Dad concludes. "Now, your mother and I have agreed that you can still babysit tomorrow night, because you've already made a commitment to Mrs. Vangraff."

"Yes," Mom adds. "She may not be able to find another babysitter on such short notice. But that will be the only place you're allowed to go for two weeks."

"Okay." Andy hasn't texted me about the dance anyway. Maybe he found out I turned him in.

"Ryan will be grounded, too, for helping you," Mom says. "For three days."

What? I feel terrible—a horrible sinking feeling. He's grounded because of me. Not to mention the fact that I used all his money to buy more flour babies.

They both stand up.

"There's something else," I say, quickly, before they can leave.

"Yes, Lizzy?"

"I knew Harrison liked me and I was mean to him. I think that's why he took my flour babies. I know you've said for us to be nice to everyone, Dad, but I didn't like him. How was I supposed to act?" "

He sits down again. "Well, when I told you to be nice to everyone, I guess I meant to be kind and cordial to everyone. That doesn't mean you have to be best friends with someone you don't want to be close to. I'm glad you're asking these questions. You're allowed not to hang out with him. You're allowed to set boundaries. Does that answer your question?"

I nod. "I guess I was trying to be too literal about what you said, Dad."

"I'm glad we've had a chance to talk about it," Dad says. "Did Harrison get detention?"

"I don't know. He wasn't in Biology. Kelly thinks he's the one who did the pranks. I saw him leaving after school with his parents."

"Well, we might not find out who did it, but meanwhile, what *he* did taking your flour babies was wrong, Lizzy, and there should be consequences."

"I told Ms. Robinson about it. She was really nice to me. She could have probably sent me to the office, or called you guys, but she didn't. She did give me a zero on the Health assignment, though. The thing is, even though Harrison took my flour babies, and I kind of hate him, I also feel sorry for him. People tease him. They put gum and sticky notes on his backpack, they give him wedgies, and they make fun of him. And I've watched guys do that to him and maybe I didn't do as much as I should have. From now on, I will."

Dad nods. "You have a good heart, Lizzy," he says. He leans against the door frame. "What about that boy that you had a crush on? Were you ever able to determine if that young man was earnest?"

"What boy?" Mom says, looking from one of us to the other.

"Oh, a guy in my Health class. I talked to Dad about it."

"You talked to Dad?" Mom says, her palm to her chest. "Not to me?"

"You told me I had to have an M.D. or a Ph.D. before I kissed a guy. I was afraid to ask you, Mom."

"Lizzy, that was just an expression, I want you to talk to me! Of course I want you to talk to me!"

I look from Mom to Dad, confused. "I didn't think you did, Mom."

"I was flattered that she came to me, Ellen."

Mom sits down on my bed. "Wayne, you can leave, I can talk to Lizzy about this."

"But first I need to find out if the young man was earnest," Dad says.

"Oh...he definitely is earnest. He's the one I helped with the camera. He's the one who caught the prankers," I tell Dad. "But you gave me good advice."

"What advice?" Mom demands.

"I told her to make sure the young man was earnest. Like in *The Importance of Being Earnest*."

"That old play? What kind of advice is that, Wayne?"

"But Ellen! It's where we met."

"I know, and I wouldn't trade it for the world. It was when we fell in love. But that play—"

"Don't say anything more, Ellen! I want to keep that memory pristine. Good night, Lizzy. Keep me posted."

Should I tell Dad that I turned Andy in?

Before I can decide, Dad runs his fingertips over the top of my head, squeezes Mom's shoulder, and leaves my room.

"So...I'm sorry, Lizzy." Mom puts her hand on my knee. "I've been distracted lately because of the job situation, and I admit to being angry with you last weekend about forgetting that interview message. But I do want to hear about things in your life. I do want you to feel that you can talk to me."

"I just..." I trace the pattern of a daisy on my bedspread. Mom has decorated my whole room with flowers. "I liked this guy...and I guess he asked me to help him, to do things that I wouldn't normally do. And, because I liked him, I did them.

And...well, I guess the school might have emailed you. I had to go to after school detention."

Mom's mouth drops open. "After school detention?"

"Yes, because he asked me to create a distraction during one of the evacuations. And then, after we went to dinner at the Mexican restaurant, he asked me to sneak out and deliver something for him and I did."

"You snuck out on Wednesday night? After Dad and I were asleep?"

I nod. "He asked me to deliver something and that's where I was going on my bike. Since I couldn't do it then, I went after you and Dad went to bed. I didn't sneak out to see him or anything—just to deliver a memory card. A policeman named Officer Egan brought me home."

"A policeman!" Mom looks like she's having heart palpitations. "I cannot believe that, Lizzy. That you did those things! I'm adding another two weeks to your grounding! You're grounded for a month!"

"Mom, you said you wanted to hear about my life and I told you and all you did was ground me."

Mom touches her mouth, as if she wishes she had never said what she said. "I'm just shocked that you would be doing all this in secret, Lizzy."

"Maybe because I'm afraid."

"I don't want you to be afraid, Lizzy. I'm sorry if I made you feel that way. You're supposed to be able to come to me at times like this and you didn't feel like you could. I was very stressed about the job situation and I let you down this week."

I keep tracing that daisy to keep myself from crying.

"Dad and I will talk about the sneaking out. And I have to tell you, I think about what a gentleman your father was when I met him during that play. Someone who really loves you will never ask you to compromise yourself. Someone who really loves you would never ask you to do something that would get you sent to detention." She takes my chin and looks into my eyes. "Do you believe me?"

"I guess. I don't think he meant to get me in trouble."

"Please, Lizzy, believe me when I say that I always want to hear about your life. No matter how busy and distracted I seem." Mom kisses me tenderly on the forehead. "Promise?"

"Promise."

After she leaves, Penelope starts crying again. I'm crying a little bit, too.

Somehow, I feel I know what she needs, and I insert the key labeled "Sleep." I clutch Penelope against my chest and rock her.

Amazingly, miraculously, she stops crying.

CHAPTER SIXTEEN

"AND HERE IS where I've put Casey's bottles." Mrs. Vangraff opens the refrigerator and points to two bottles lined in a compartment inside the door. "He will need one to be warmed just a little—not too much, the way I showed you—at about six o'clock, and another one at eight, right before bed. Be sure and burp him after he eats. You know how to burp a baby, don't you, Lizzy?" She looks at me and smiles, raising her eyebrows hopefully. She's wearing a silk outfit in a wild shade of green. Her make-up and perfume smell airy and fabulous. I wonder if I should apologize again for grabbing her boobs in the restaurant and decide it's best not to bring it up.

"Yes, I know how to burp him." I'm holding Casey on my hip and so far he has sucked and slobbered on his fingers and now he's smearing them all over my face. There is no sign whatsoever of colic, thank the lord. Even though I did do about twenty Google searches to be prepared.

"Honey, ready to go?" Mr. Vangraff stands by the front

door, one hand on the doorknob, the other jiggling the car keys in his hand. He wears a peach shirt with a flower pattern. When he opened the door on my arrival, I smelled cologne on him, too.

And may I say, they both seem *pretty excited* to be getting out of the house.

"Yes, I'm just giving Lizzy last-minute instructions." Mrs. Vangraff picks up her purse, points to phone numbers she's written on a Post-It on the refrigerator door. "Both our cell phones. Now, we'll have to turn them off during the play, but don't hesitate to call if you need to, and we'll give you a call during intermission to make sure everything is all right."

"OK."

"Lizzy, is your mom at home tonight?"

"Yes, ma'am. If anything happens, she can come right over."

"Wonderful. You seem as though you have things well in hand. I know you're responsible and I trust you, especially with your mom just down the street."

They think I'm responsible. They trust me. Casey's weight is warm against my hip. I smile confidently. "OK. Bye!" I take Casey's sloppy starfish hand and wave good-bye to them. And, like bank robbers making a getaway, they duck out the front door.

"OK, Casey," I say. "It's just you and me." He stares at me with his mouth hanging open, breathes heavily, with a loud congested sound, and tries to lick my cheek.

Well, actually, it's me and Casey and Penelope. I brought her in my backpack, so Mrs. Vangraff wouldn't think I was taking time away from Casey to take care of her. Mrs. Vangraff has shown me Casey's toys and books, which are scattered on the coffee table and around the family room floor. Casey seems pretty calm. He seems to like me, especially touching my face or pulling my long hair with his slobbery fingers.

It makes me feel good that Casey likes me. I mean, he's a

baby, he's met—what?—twenty people in his whole life, so how critical can he be? But still, it makes me feel good.

I give Casey a bottle, right at six, and then I carefully pat his soft little back until he lets go with a wet belch that ricochets off the walls. We play paddy cake, and we play peek-a-boo. We watch Baby Mozart. I read him *Goodnight Moon* about fifty times. Every time he sees that grandmother in the rocking chair he squeals and I wonder, does he like her, or does she scare him a little bit, the way she scares me?

I pick him up and carry him around on my hip and I must tell you he feels NOTHING like Ziggy did. There's no comparison. Sure, he's wiggly and squirmy. But he's warm and his skin feels so amazing and he *hugs* you. If you poke your finger in his belly button he gives a squeal that just makes you laugh. He's *so* much better.

The main thing that worries me is the soft spot. While I'm carrying him I run my fingers over the top of his head and feel the silky hair covering that soft place right in the middle. It seems so tender there.

I try not to let myself think about what Andy's doing. I don't let myself wonder who danced with him last night.

I take care of Casey. That's what I'm here for. It's serious. Tonight, I am going to prove I'm responsible. This is a REAL BABY.

Penelope, blessedly, is quiet. She started crying before I came over here and I picked the correct key the first time—call me crazy, I think I'm getting to know her—and she quieted right down.

At seven-forty-five, Mrs. Vangraff calls. "Hi, Lizzy, how's it going? The play is starting in fifteen minutes and I just wanted to call and check before we go in."

I tell her that everything is great. Because it is. He hasn't cried once.

Right at eight, I give him the second bottle, burp him, change his diaper, then I put on his amazingly adorable PJs with little cartoon animals on them, and lay him in his crib on his side, as Mrs. Vangraff instructed. I turn on the musical toy hanging over his crib and he waves his arms and legs around with excitement as he watches it go around and around.

Mrs. Vangraff explained that I shouldn't stay in the room after that, that I should get the baby monitor and walk right out, even if he cries. But the thing is, he grabs my finger. And his eyelids sink lower and lower while he chews on the end of my finger and it has taken me no time at all not to mind his slobber, and so I just stand there, hanging over the crib, letting him grip my finger and gnaw on the end with his sharp little gums.

And when he falls asleep it's sudden. His eyes close, he takes a breath, and his fingers unfurl like flower petals.

I inch my finger free, run my palm lightly, once more, over the top of his head, over his tender soft spot, and back out of the room. I leave the door just slightly ajar, and tiptoe down the stairs with the baby monitor.

For a few minutes I sit on the couch, first making sure the monitor is working right, then just thinking back over everything. With a real baby there's so much hugging and touching and the feel of your skin right next to the baby's skin and then there's the lovely way he smells. I'm tired but I just feel overflowing with love. It's hard to put into words.

I think I would be a good mom. Maybe I forgot my flour babies, but there is no way I'd forget a *real* one.

I start picking up the toys, because Mom reminded me that Mrs. Vangraff would practically kiss my feet if I did that. Then I put away the dishes.

Unable to help myself, I tiptoe back upstairs.

I want to go in the room and look at Casey, feast my eyes on his fat little cheeks and half-open wet bow mouth. I think I could smell his baby smell and get high. Maybe I can tiptoe in without waking him up.

No, better not.

Back downstairs, I text Marisa and I ask her if Andy hung out with anyone at the dance last night.

He wasn't there, she texts back.

Really?

So why not? Has he been expelled? My brain begins its typical Andy whirl.

And that's when I get another text. From Andy.

I break into a sudden sweat. He seems to be a few blocks away, spending the night with Billy Z. He says he just got his phone back from his dad and wants to know where I am and what I'm doing.

Goosebumps race from my scalp all the way down my back.

Deduction: He does not know I turned him in. Otherwise he would hate me for life and would not be calling me.

Figuring this out makes relief flow through my body like warm water.

So, where was he last night?

I'm babysitting, I type back.

The empty house hums around me.

I just put the baby to sleep.

I pretend not to know about last night.

Was the dance fun?

At last he responds: **Didn't go. Grounded. Long story I need to tell you. How far away are you?**

I hesitate. Long story? About what? My heart pounds when I type in the address, and, a few minutes later, when I see him through the sliding glass door on the back deck, I almost scream because with the porch light shining down on the top of his head he looks like a ghoul. I know I've made a mistake when I slide open the door to let him in. When he steps into the light it's shocking—his face seems giant and balloon-like after Casey's, with huge pores and thick hairs sprouting above his lip and on his chin.

His teeth gleam in the half-light and I think of Jack Sparrow from *Pirates of the Caribbean*.

"Hey, Tin Lizzy." When he reaches to squeeze the back of my neck the way he always does, Andy's hand looks gargantuan, hairy and long-fingered like an ape. "Thin Lizzy."

"Maybe you shouldn't be here." I should never have done this. This is not responsible."

"I won't stay long."

I walk back into the room where the light is on and he comes with me, his arm loosely looped over my shoulders. "So... you didn't go to the dance?" I ask. My voice sounds like a little kid.

"No. My dad grounded me from the dance yesterday afternoon when he found out I got out of going to detention." A warm little quiver races from my belly button to my throat. He sits on the couch, checks his phone, puts it away, stands up, and sits down again. He points at me, then pats the couch next to him. "Come sit with me."

"You know, Andy, this doesn't feel right." I cross my arms over my chest and stand halfway across the room from him, fighting AMSD, trying to get far enough away that I can't feel the gravitational pull.

"Let me just tell you what happened," he says. "After we went back inside and everyone went back to Health class, I went to the office to get my camera back, and they were playing the tape. They didn't plan on letting me know who did it, but I figured it out."

"Who?"

"A guy named Brian Williams, do you know him? And he

had help from a kid in the computer club named Gordon."

My mouth drops open. Brian Williams! The guy who called me Lizzy Borden! "Yeah. I was in detention with him. And Gordon sits behind us on the bus!"

"Yeah. Lance had done some cartoons of some of the teachers, and Brian took them without Lance knowing. He had figured out Mr. Waggoner's login information, just by asking Mr. Waggoner a bunch of questions about his favorite teams and stuff, and then used some kind of software that spoofed his identity. They used his login to get access to a bunch of other teachers' login information, including Mr. Hanson, the head of maintenance, then used Mr. Hanson's logins to access the HVAC system and set up the fire drills. The reason they went back to the computer lab that last time was to try to cover their tracks. They'd forgotten to take their own names out of the file. I got him recorded that last time after you and I taped the camera on the loudspeaker, and when they interviewed him, he admitted to everything else. Mr. Joya figured out that the reason we had that last fire drill was because one of the teachers had just gone on maternity leave, and didn't change her password."

"So...it wasn't Harrison?"

"Nope."

My heart squeezes. A jumble of emotions flood me. Anger. Guilt. Regret. Relief. For a long minute, I can't say anything. I picture Harrison's thin pale face, his straight hair, his tortoiseshell glasses, his sour smell as he poked his head between Kelly and me on the bus. I guess the only thing Harrison did was steal my flour babies.

Finally, I say, "I thought it might be him, since he missed the Biology test. And then later I saw him leaving the school with his parents while I was waiting for Ryan."

"I heard them talking about it in the office," Andy says. "His parents moved him to another school."

"Really?" So that was what happened. This news makes me feel oddly sad.

"They said he wasn't happy at our school."

"Oh, he definitely wasn't," I say, feeling guilty once again for not standing up for him more.

My heart races as I try to decide whether I'll tell Andy that I turned him in.

"I figured Lance did the caricatures," I say. "But it's a relief to know he wasn't actually involved."

As we sit in silence, letting this sink it, I think about Lance in detention, and how he seemed to be quietly seething with anger, and how Brian jostled his arm while he was drawing his dragon.

Then I think about my own interview, and how scared I was, and about what I said to Mrs. J about Andy. I have a strong desire to come clean with Andy, to tell him I turned him in, but I press my lips together. I'm afraid to tell him. Now I don't even know why I did it.

"The cops interviewed me," he says, "but I showed them all my interviews, and they saw that I didn't have anything to hide. So, everything was cool." Andy searches my face. "So now you and I are kind of secret heroes."

I have a twinge in my gut, but it's overtaken by the return of my acute case of AMSD.

He picks up *Good Night Moon*. "Come on, Busy Lizzy, let's read a story."

"Have you ever read it?"

"My mom read it to me every night when I was a baby."

"Really?"

He nods. "I have it memorized. Sit beside me, Dizzy Lizzy. I'll read it to you."

Feeling like a melting popsicle, I walk over and sit next to him on the Vangraff's micro suede couch. I sit about a foot away but somehow the electromagnetism really goes crazy and two seconds later our thighs are touching underneath the book.

Without opening the book he recites, "There's a tiny little old lady yelling at us to 'hush!'"

AMSD takes hold and I start to laugh. "That's not it—you skipped practically the whole thing!"

"I know, sorry," he says quickly. He turns his eyes on me and our faces move closer.

Goosebumps prick their way up my spine.

"I'm sorry I got you in trouble," he says, his lips hovering close to mine.

I could say, "I almost got you in trouble, too," but I don't.

"That's OK," I say, feeling the warmth of his breath on my skin. I hear Mom's voice in my head. *Someone who loves you would never make you compromise who you are.*

"I get so excited about getting a story," he adds, "I forget to think about some of the consequences."

As he says "consequences," my lips touch the soft dry skin of his. We have both stopped breathing. I feel a little disoriented, like Dorothy lost in the field of poppies in the *Wizard of Oz*.

Is he earnest? comes Dad's voice in my head.

I pull my lips away, and it's like fighting the bonds of superglue or the gravity of Alpha Centauri. "Are you earnest?"

"What?" Andy blinks and focuses his eyes on me, as if coming back from very far away.

"We better stop," I say.

And then there's a bleating, insistent cry.

"What's that?" Andy jumps.

Is Casey awake? I jump to my feet. The wailing escalates.

"Oh, no! It's Penelope!" I sprint around the couch and dig through my purse and then wonder what I did with her keys and think that maybe I left them at home. Could I have really done that? I realize with horror: Yes, I could.

I dump my purse out on the floor, sending pens and lip gloss rolling across the slick hardwood. Penelope's wailing grows louder.

"That's the most annoying sound I ever heard," Andy says.

As if Penelope yowling isn't bad enough, now the phone starts ringing. It must be intermission. Or Mom, checking on me.

Andy picks up Penelope and holds her rubber doll face close to his. "And I'm asking you to *hush!*" he says firmly. She wails louder. He stuffs her under one of the couch cushions. Her muffled cries continue.

I hold my finger over my lips, grab the phone and run to the dining room to answer. "Vangraff Residence."

"Hi, Lizzy, it's Mrs. Vangraff. It's intermission, how's everything going?"

"Just great! He's asleep."

"Do I hear him crying? Everyone here in the theater lobby is talking, I can't hear that well."

"No, no, he's not crying. Casey is fast asleep."

"Are you sure? It seems like there's crying."

"That's not Casey. That's my mechanical baby for school."

"Really? I didn't know you had a mechanical baby for school."

"Yeah. She was in my backpack."

"Really." She sounds like she's light years from believing me.

"Really."

"So everything is fine?"

"Just fine."

When she hangs up, I race back into the family room, my heart in my throat. This is a disaster! Andy must have been trying to listen to the mechanism inside Penelope because now one of the buttons on her pajamas has caught on the back of his earring.

"Get her off of me!" he yells. "But be careful with my earlobe. This is my favorite earring. Plus I can't stand the sight of blood."

"OK, just hold still!" Leaning close to him, smelling his hair, with the mechanical baby wailing between us, my heart beats triple-time and I think my head is going to explode. Finally I get the button free, and while Andy piles cushions on top of Penelope, I hurry behind the couch and search frantically through the contents of my purse on the floor. No keys.

My brain leaps into hyper speed. Who can help me?

Ryan.

I need to get Andy out of here with Penelope fast so she doesn't wake Casey.

A muffled cry wavers from the baby monitor.

Too late. Now what?

"Maybe I better take off," Andy tries to hand me Penelope, who now sounds like an entire herd of sick goats. He skips backward toward the glass sliding door with a nervous laugh.

"What?" I say. "You're going to leave in the middle of all this?" I stare at him in disbelief.

"Well, what do you want me to do?" He throws his arms in the air helplessly, then claps his palms over his ears.

I shove Penelope into his arms. "You *have* to help me."

"Um...okay," he says.

"I've got to go upstairs and get Casey." I leap up the stairs. "Call Ryan and ask him to meet you on our back deck with Penelope's keys. His number is on my contacts list." I toss my phone over the stair banister, in his direction.

Juggling Penelope, Andy lunges for it.

Upstairs, Casey roars like a stuck hippopotamus. I lean over the crib, scoop him up, and hold him close. His trembling wet face is against my neck, and his cries go on. Between sobs, I hear the sliding door downstairs squeal shut.

Andy is gone.

Casey's face glows red, and he's soaked with sweat with the effort of his crying. His damp red curls are glued to his head. I bounce around the room the way I've seen Mrs. Vangraff do. My heart pounds and I know Casey can feel it. I tell myself to be calm, that he will be calm if I am.

"Shhh, it's OK," I whisper, trying to believe that myself.

Ten minutes later it's not any better and my eardrums pound with all the screaming. Finally I put him back in the crib and call Mom.

"Wow, I can hear him from here," she says. "Just remember, babies generally are not going to hurt themselves by crying. Try sitting in the rocking chair with him and giving him a little bit more of the bottle," she says. "And don't forget to burp him afterward. If that doesn't work, call me back and I'll come over."

I get the last bit of the last bottle and sit in the rocking chair in Casey's bedroom with him on my lap. I whisper, "Hush." He grabs the bottle like he hasn't eaten in weeks. Five minutes later his head lolls back and his mouth drops open in sleep.

I sit there for a minute or so, totally amazed at how quickly this has happened. I burp him, and then I rock, waiting for my heart to slow down and my head to stop pounding. I call Mom and whisper to her. "It worked. He's asleep. Thanks, Mom."

"Oh, good, honey, I'm glad. You did well," she says. "Bye. Love you!" Hearing those words from her is like feeling golden sunlight on my face. But if she knew Andy had been over here, what would she say then?

———

A few minutes later, Andy knocks on the sliding door, and I let him in. He has a quiet Penelope in his arms. I hold my finger over my lips to shush him.

"Ryan and I were on your back deck, trying all the keys," he stage whispers. "It was pretty funny. 'Feed' finally worked."

"Thanks for doing that." He follows me inside as I take Penelope and put her on the couch.

"So..." he says, touching my arm. "I better go. You were right, Thin Lizzy, this wasn't the best idea. I don't want to get you in trouble again."

At that moment the grinding sound of the Vangraff's' garage door assaults our ears.

"Oh, no! They're home early!" I clap my hand over my mouth. I run over to the door to the garage and hold my ear up close. "You've got to go!"

Andy gasps. He trips over the rug by the couch while running to the sliding door and sprawls on the floor, then clambers back to his feet and struggles to get the door to open.

"Hurry!" I say.

We finally wrench the door open and Andy fumbles out onto their back deck and practically falls down the stairs as he runs.

"I'll meet you by my swing set!" I say, seconds before the Vangraffs walk into the kitchen from the garage. The backyard motion detector lights flash on like sweeping beams from a UFO and Andy is illuminated as he leaps over their fence and disappears into the trees at the edge of their yard.

"You're home early! Did you have fun?" I say, leaning casually against the couch, holding my breath, not sure if they have seen him.

"Why is our motion detector on?" asks Mrs. Vangraff.

"I—um," I'm sure they can see my heart pounding in my chest.

Mr. Vangraff goes out onto the back deck and surveys the

back yard. "Probably just that stray cat that's been coming around," he says as he comes back in.

"I got worried about the crying I heard in the background when I talked to you," says Mrs. Vangraff. "I told my husband we needed to go home."

"We missed the last act," says Mr. Vangraff. "I never did get to see if Ernest got Gwendolyn after revealing that his name was really Jack."

"Was the play *The Importance of Being Earnest?*" I ask with amazement.

"Yes, do you know it?" Mrs. Vangraff says.

"Sort of," I say. "And don't worry, it turns out that his nanny lost him in a handbag and Jack was his adoptive name. The name his real parents gave him was Ernest. So Gwendolyn can marry him."

"His nanny lost him in a handbag?" asks Mr. Vangraff, puzzled.

"Yes."

"It was a kind of silly play," says Mrs. Vangraff.

"Anyway, the crying was Penelope," I show her. "Casey is upstairs asleep."

"I need to check."

My kneecaps tremble as I follow Mrs. Vangraff upstairs and she peers into his quiet bedroom. She tiptoes over to the crib and gazes at the sleeping baby for a long quiet moment. "Well, he certainly is," she says. She turns and looks at me and smiles. "And the house is so neat and tidy. I can't tell you how wonderful that is. You are such a responsible girl, Lizzy. Thank you."

As we're coming back downstairs, I pick up my backpack and then stop short. Andy's backpack is also there, lying beside the couch.

Can I grab them both without Mrs. Vangraff noticing?

I start to swoop them both up and she says, "Why do you have two backpacks, Lizzy?"

"Uh—"

I must have a guilty look on my face because she crosses her arms and gives me a cold stare. "Did someone come over here? Is that why the motion detector was on?"

"Uh—" I think about lying but I have lied enough this week. "Yes, ma'am."

She looks at me in a totally new way. All of a sudden the respect she had for me is gone. But she doesn't yell at me. She just says very quietly, "We left our precious baby boy in your care."

"But you can trust me. I took perfect care of him—"

"I'm disappointed in you, Lizzy. We did not give you permission to have a friend over. I'll pay you for tonight but we won't be calling you again."

She thrusts a few bills at me and holds the front door open. I drag myself out with the two backpacks. The door slams behind me.

I feel like crying. I kind of fell in love with Casey tonight. Now I'll never babysit for him again.

———

I trudge home under the low-hanging trees and spot Andy on our backyard swing set. He has done that thing where he twists the swing tighter and tighter, and then lets himself go, twirling in faster and faster circles as he unwinds. That's sort of the way I feel about this week. It's completely spun out of control.

I can't help but love watching him, so kid-like and innocent. Everything about him thrills me. Just being around him is like plugging into some magic power grid. He whirls to a stop, his shoes skidding in the dust.

The thrill fades a little. I have to tell him. My steps slow as I approach.

"Dizzy Miss Lizzy," he says.

"Here's your backpack. It gave you away."

He reaches out and takes it. "What do you mean?"

"They figured out you were there and I admitted it. They said they won't be calling me again."

"Oh! Bummer." It occurs to me that since he's not affected, he doesn't seem to care that much. And that bothers me.

"There's one thing I didn't tell you," I say.

"What a coincidence. There's one thing I didn't tell you," he says.

"You go first."

"Okay...I'm the one that set off the firecracker in the Dumpster."

"What?" My jaw drops. I feel myself flushed with anger when I hear his words. "You did that? Andy, people were hurt. Chelsea's arm was bleeding and could have been broken. Marisa and I got trampled. Do you know how scared everyone was? We thought it was a *school shooting*."

He pauses, my words taking him by surprise. When he speaks, he sounds defensive. "Yeah, but it was in the soccer field Dumpster, it was too far away for anyone to really get hurt. Besides, it was like the ultimate April Fools' prank. It was such a rush. And it was a form of protest, too. The administration should do better. And I knew after I'd solved everything else no one would suspect me." He shrugs. "I guess I didn't think about people stampeding."

I look at his face and feel so confused. I see him in a different light now. Just like Mrs. Vangraff saw me in a different light after she knew about Andy's visit. Some of the glow around Andy has disappeared. "Setting off that firecracker—

that was like a terrorist or something. Andy, we were terrified. A lot of us were hurt!"

"Stop yelling at me! I thought you would understand!"

"What if someone had been killed, Andy?" I am starting to shake, I'm so mad. How can he not see how wrong he was to do that?

"You sound like my parents!"

"Andy, that was a terrible thing to do!"

Finally he looks down at the ground. "Okay, I did it. It was a terrible thing to do. But it's over now and we're lucky nothing worse happened." He looks back up at me. "Your turn. What thing did you not tell me?"

Now what I have to say doesn't even seem that important. After all, I did something I thought was right. But I take a deep breath. He's been honest with me, so I should be honest with him. "When the principal interviewed me, I told her about going to Billy Z's house with the memory chip."

"That's OK," he says. "Getting interviewed is scary. Plus, they saw that there was nothing on it but the Chief's interview."

"There's more." I think that I can't look at him, but I do. Right at him. "I sent an anonymous email. I turned you in. I thought you might have done it."

I brace myself for his response.

"You turned me in?" he says. Our porch light reflects the disbelief in his eyes.

I wish I had never done it. But does he wish he'd never set off the firecracker?

"You had been late to class," I say. "And you seemed so excited about the pranks making it a better news week, and I have no doubt you're good enough on a computer to pull something like that off. Not to mention the fact that you're in the computer club. And you have Billy Z's help any time you need it. And everyone was telling me about my civic duty. And, well, I thought you were ghosting me. I know now I was wrong, because your dad took—"

"When you came to my house you seemed like you might suspect me, but then I thought I'd convinced you I wasn't involved. After all that, you still thought I did it?" His eyes are hot with anger. "They told me someone turned me in...but never in a million years would I have thought it was you!"

I sigh. "I thought I was doing the right thing."

"God, Lizzy! I thought I could trust you!"

"What about me trusting you? What I did was harmless as long as you were able to prove you weren't involved. I got turned in, too, for your information. By Harrison. And I ended up being able to prove I didn't do anything. But what you did hurt people. You don't think about how your actions affect other people. Like babysitting. You coming over meant I can't babysit for Casey any more. But you don't really care because it doesn't affect you."

"It was your decision too, Lizzy!"

I can't believe he's turning this back around on me. But he's right about one thing: I made a decision. I had a choice. I just glare at him. My eyes are beginning to burn with tears.

"Are you going to tell them about the firecracker now?" he says.

"I don't know. I can't believe you didn't care about me getting into trouble. All you care about is whether I'm going to tell on you." I'm crying now, hot angry tears. "You should tell them yourself."

He jerks away from me and then launches himself from the swing, leaving it creaking in the night air. He stomps across our yard, and I know I've made him angry. I don't try to follow. I hear the rasp of his kickstand and the whirr of his bicycle tires on the asphalt.

Tears roll down my cheeks, faster and faster. I sob until my nose is running and my eyes swell up and my head pounds. How could I have spent this week liking him so much? I'm furious at him, but I don't want to see him go. I don't want to think about not seeing him anymore.

How can I still be so attracted to him, when I now know what he did?

It feels like the end of the world.

————

Thirty minutes later, I tiptoe past Mom and Dad's closed door and walk soundlessly into Ryan's room. He's online in the dark, the only light a bluish glow from his computer screen. I cradle Penelope in my arms.

"God," he says when he looks at me. "You look like your entire face got stung by a bee."

"Thanks. Your glasses are smeared." I sniffle. My head hurts too much to cry anymore. If I blow my nose again I'll probably burst a blood vessel and bleed to death.

"Have you been crying?"

"Yeah."

"What about?"

"Nothing."

He stares at me in silence for long seconds, then seems to decide not to press it. "You owe me," he says. "Big time."

"I know." I hand him some of the money I made from babysitting. "Thanks for buying all of those flour babies."

He stares at me.

"I'm sorry I got you grounded."

"Me, too. Did they ever see Mr. Pomme Frite?"

I sigh and pat Penelope on the back. "Yeah. They said they won't be calling me again."

"What were you thinking?"

"I don't know. I wasn't." I sit at the foot of his bed, just listening to the sound of the air moving in and out of me as minutes spin by. I watch Ryan's back as he types, noticing the scalloped line of ribs showing through his T-shirt along his long thin back.

He looks out the window and we're silent for a while.

"Guys are weird," I say at last. "Opposite sex stuff, it's weird."

"Lizzy, what did you do?" Ryan stops staring out the window and turns around. His hair is awry.

"We kissed."

His face relaxes, and I think he believes me. "I said some bad things about him before, and I should take those back, because he didn't seem like a bad guy. He was pretty freaked over Penelope crying. He really didn't want you mad at him. He said he wanted to interview me for *The WLHS Show*."

"What about?"

"What you should do starting as a freshman to build a resume for being yearbook editor."

"Oh." I'm quite sure Andy will be yearbook editor his senior year.

"But you should never have let him come over while you were babysitting."

"I know. It was stupid." I stand and turn to leave, but then lie back on his bed. "I thought he was the most exciting person. But it turns out he wasn't who I thought he was."

Ryan looks at me through his smeared lenses. "Lizzy, it's hard to really know a person."

I think about the fact that Andy probably thought he knew me. He thought he could trust me. "Ryan, I turned him in that night when we talked."

"I didn't know that. Was it because of what I said?"

"Maybe, partially. Also, he stopped texting me, and I

thought he was ghosting me, and my feelings were hurt. But that ended up being because his dad took his phone. And tonight, I felt like I had to tell him. I had to be honest. And now he won't speak to me. But meanwhile, he *did* do something bad. And, to be honest, I'm not too sure how I feel about him now."

"Oh." Ryan stares.

"Ryan, he's the one who set off the firecracker in the Dumpster."

Ryan slaps his forehead with his hand, then stares at me in silence. Then, he finally says, "That's unbelievable! He did that? What a bonehead! It could have been so dangerous! He would be expelled for that."

"I know. It's just made me see him in a completely different way. He doesn't think about other people."

"Maybe at your fortieth high school reunion you'll go up to each other and say you forgive each other."

"Maybe. I don't know, Ryan."

He tosses a Star Wars action figure of Han Solo in the air and catches it. "Who knows, maybe you'll visit him in Alcatraz."

"Ryan! It's not funny."

Tears start to well in my eyes again. I wipe them away.

"You really thought he was involved," he said, "so you did the right thing."

"He *was* involved." I sigh and stand to go. "Ryan, the very least you can do is clean your darned glasses."

He tiredly removes his glasses, breathes to fog them, and polishes them with the end of his T-shirt.

"Thanks for giving Andy Penelope's key. Good night, Ryan. Love you."

"Night, Lizzy. Love you, too."

I go into my bedroom and lay Penelope on the extra pillow so I can get ready for bed. She's probably going to cry again soon.

Under the covers, I pull her close to me. Outside my window, the full moon splashes silvery blue light across the little girl furniture in my room.

My mind rolls back over all that has happened over the past week. All the stuff I did, stuff that I had never dreamed of doing before. My week of infamy.

If I had it all to do over again, would I?

I get up and go in the bathroom and examine my foreign face in the mirror. The red tissue under my eyelids. The way my gums turn white if I poke them. The huge pores in the corners of my nose. My freshman year of high school will be over in a few months. In one week I got kicked out of the cheerleading competition, sent to detention, received both a zero and an F, got followed by a cop, was nearly suspended, was fired from a babysitting job, and gained and lost a boyfriend.

Have I morphed into a monster? Did having that crush on Andy turn me into a pod person?

No, it didn't. The moment I think it, I know that's not the answer. I'm not a bad person. Maybe I made some mistakes. But if you don't take risks and make mistakes, then you don't learn. Deep down, I know that. There is more to life than getting straight As.

Like with the hackers, there are the white hats and the black hats. There are also a lot of gray hats. Good guys aren't good all the time, bad guys aren't bad all the time, and people make mistakes. I made mistakes. Andy made mistakes. Mom poked a hole in the wall at work, so she made a mistake, too. People aren't perfect, and what's more, we shouldn't be.

So what am I going to do? I'm going to pick myself up and, just as Mrs. Cruz said, do better.

Before I go to bed, there is one thing I want to do. I turn on my computer and go to my email.

. . .

Dear Harrison,

Thank you for the incredibly detailed notes on the dissection that you shared with Kelly and me.

I'm sorry the boys on the bus bullied you. Good luck at your new school.

Lizzy

I turn off the computer and climb into bed. I think about how it will be when I pass Andy in the hall next week. Maybe we will pretend that we never met. It could take a long time to get over AMSD—no known cure.

My head tells me that he's not the boy I thought I knew, and I don't feel the same as I did last Friday, when he sang "Skinny Love" all off-key and asked for my number.

However, in my heart, it doesn't feel like knowing what he's really like has cured anything. I still care about him. I still have that electric feeling when I think of Andy. So it's just made things more complicated. But maybe that's a start.

Andy will always be my first crush. Maybe the cure that my heart needs is something else entirely. As my role model Dr. Sharon Parker has always said, "Healing needs tincture of time." And, after some time has passed, who knows?

I will be sixteen in a few months. I think about the rest of this year, this summer, and the next. Camp Med. AP Biology. Varsity Cheerleading. Driving to school instead of riding the bus. Three more years of April Fools' week. New friends. New responsibilities. Maybe a job volunteering at the hospital.

Just as I predicted, Penelope starts to cry. I get out the key that says "Change."

I turn it, and Penelope stops.

ACKNOWLEDGMENTS

I worked on this book on and off for a long time and many people helped me with it.

Heartfelt thanks to...

...my treasured writer friends who read, commented and kept me going, including Ann Campanella, Nancy Lammers, Carolyn Noell, Ruth Ann Grissom, Judy Stacy, Jean Beatty, Liz Hatley, Kimmery Martin, Emily Smith Pearce, Betsy Thorpe, Margaret Nevinski and Nancy Thalia Reynolds, among others. I feel so lucky to be part of this writing community.

...Lorin Oberweger and Nancy Lamb for their editorial expertise.

...Edgar Joya, who talked with me about computer hacking.

...Katy Patterson, who talked with me about school evacuations.

...Mira Pearce, who has read my books before and kindly read this one and gave me invaluable ninth grade advice.

...Katie Rose Guest Pryal and Lauren Faulkenberry for choosing this story for Goldenjay Books.

...Lauren Faulkenberry and Katie Guest Pryal for their

insightful editing, vision, and crucial encouragement. What a gift to have writers as editors!

...my daughters Caitlin and Kelsey for their constant inspiration.

...my husband Jeff whose support and love I am grateful for every day.

ABOUT THE AUTHOR

Lisa Williams Kline is the author of nine novels for young people, including *Princesses of Atlantis* (Carus), *Write Before Your Eyes* (Delacorte), the five-book *Sisters in All Seasons* series (Zondervan), and *Eleanor Hill* (Carus), which won the North Carolina Juvenile Literature Award.

Kline is also author of a collection of short stories for adults entitled *Take Me* (Main Street Rag). She is a winner of the Press 53 Short Story Contest and won Honorable Mention in the *Glimmer Train* Winter Fiction Open.

A graduate of Duke University, she has a masters degree in Radio, Television, and Film from UNC-Chapel Hill, and an MFA from Queens University. She has served as president of the Charlotte Writers' Club, is a former board member of the North Carolina Writers' Network, is a mentor in the SCBWI Mentor Program, and critiques manuscripts for Writers' Digest. She lives in North Carolina with her veterinarian husband, Jeff, and numerous spoiled pets. Their two daughters visit frequently with their dogs and—as one might imagine—they have a howling good time.

Visit her website at lisawilliamskline.com.

facebook.com/lisa.kline.566

twitter.com/LisaWKline

instagram.com/lisawilliamskline

amazon.com/author/lisakline

bookbub.com/authors/lisa-williams-kline

goodreads.com/lisa_kline

CPSIA information can be obtained
at www.ICGtesting.com
Printed in the USA
FFHW020609030319
50767964-56183FF